Eighty-nine pounds

Prologue

I wake up, rub my eyes, and brush through my tangly, curly hair. *I need to shower,* I thought as I get out of bed. I walk over to my mirror and yank off my clothes. I close my eyes, take a deep breath, and then open them again. As usual, I hate what I see. My too pale skin, my thighs that refuse to form a gap, my stomach that never loses that baby bump look, and my arm fat that jiggles slightly if I raise my arms above my head. I'm so fat, but I can't stop staring. My flaws are screaming at me all at once. My hair so curly that it looks frizzy all of the time. My crooked smile. My one eye that is only slightly smaller than the other. My torso is disproportionate from my bottom half. God, I hate myself.

I grab my workout clothes and look out the window to see who is home. The driveway is empty. I smile; no one is here. I am alone. I put on my workout clothes, and head to down to our gym in the basement. Let my two hour workout begin.

I head for the treadmill first and do my usual 5 miles. By the time I am done I'm starting to sweat, and I feel slightly dizzy. I ignore it, drink some water, and begin my sit ups. I go until my stomach is crying out in pain. I go back to the treadmill, and again ignore the dizziness that is becoming increasingly worse. My body is covered in sweat and I'm struggling to catch my breath, but I don't care. I put one foot in front of the other. I have my music blaring to drown out the pleas in brain, begging me to stop. *Shut up!* I tell my brain. *I must not stop, I need to be skinny.*

I can barely see the room, the colors are all swirling together, and the music is fading. I still keep running; I can't stop now. *Must keep going, must be skinny, must keep going...* The last thing I see is the ceiling swirl into itself before I collapse.

...

I wake up several....hours…days...months later? I have no concept of time at all. I can't open my eyes though. I hear a steady beeping noise, and faint voices. *Where am I?* I try moving my fingers, my head, my toes, but I find that I don't have the strength.

The voices are growing louder, and one of them sounds very familiar. Shrill, and full of worry. *Mom?* "How is she?" My mom asked to who ever else was in the room with us.

"Well, Emily's heart rate is back to normal, and we've hydrated her again, but we would like to keep her under observation. Specifically, a 72 hour suicide watch." said by a voice I would assume was a doctor.

"Wha- I don't understand Dr. Mills, a suicide watch?" My mother asked quietly, on the verge of tears.

"Yes, ma'am. The nurses and I have spoken excessively about this. We just need your permission to keep her here." Dr. Mills spoke calmly.

"What does...um...what does this suicide watch entail?" My mother said, her voice rising slightly.

"Well, during the seventy-two hour period, Emily will meet with a therapist, who will evaluate her. During the watch, Emily is not permitted any visitors or phone calls; part of the policy. After the seventy-two hours are over, we will call you in to discuss what would be best for Emily." Dr. Mills said firmly.

My mom sighed deeply, knowing there was no way out of this. "What will be the possible options for her after this watch?"

"That we don't know yet," said Dr. Mills "but if my hunch is correct, the likely treatment option will be a mental institution."

"I don't understand why all of this is needed." My mom said, sounding a tad bit annoyed. "Emily is fine".

"Mrs. Gerard, we don't know exactly what is wrong with Emily yet, but we do know she is very ill. All I ask for is your patience, please. Let us take care of your daughter." Dr. Mills asked, trying very hard to hide his frustration.

My mother was silent for a moment before she gave a very quiet, "Yes...alright. I understand. You said you had a hunch? May I ask what your hunch is?"

"Certainly, Mrs. Gerard. We looked over Emily's previous medical records from the past year. Her height is average for her age but her weight concerned us..." Dr. Mills said.

"What do you mean?" her voice shaking.

"Emily's last listed weight is 100 pounds when she got her check-up in August. We weighed her after we stabilized her and the scale read eighty-nine pounds." Dr. Mills said gravely.

My mom gasped, and I smiled. I was finally less than 90 pounds.

Chapter 1

"Go on," said Dr. John "You can talk to me about anything, Emily."

He handed me a tissue, as I let out another sob. I sniffled and nodded. "I'm just afraid he'll know I told you."

Dr. John looked at me with a soft expression on his face and said "He won't know you told me. He's not here with us. You must remember this."

I drew in a shaky breath, grabbed one of the pillows on the couch and hugged it to my body. Crying was making me tired, I didn't have much strength to me these days. I was still happy that I was less than ninety pounds, and I knew Darren would be happy, but he wasn't here, and it was the doctor's turn to tell me how much I needed to weigh. There was always someone who wanted me to weigh a certain amount; I can't remember the last time it was up to me.

"Emily?" Dr. John's voice was drawing me back. "I know you can do this. You've made great progress over the past two weeks."

When I was finally strong enough to move my body parts, Dr. Mills told me I would be under a suicide watch, and I would be seeing Dr. John. Of course I wasn't happy. I had to get back home and lose more weight for Darren. Unfortunately, I didn't have a choice in what was happening to me. I was too sick, and my condition was too poor.

My first meeting with Dr. John started with me in a fit of hysteria. I told him I needed to be home, I needed to lose more weight or Darren would be upset. When he asked who Darren was, I cried harder and didn't talk for the rest of the session. It was enough for the doctor's though. They at least knew someone else was involved in my problem, creating a focus point for our meetings.

The next meeting with Dr. John, we didn't talk about Darren much. I implied that he was my dance instructor, but that was it. The rest of the time he asked me about my workout schedule, and how I felt after I would work out. I told him I felt happy, of course. I could feel the calories leaving my body as my muscles burned and screamed with pain.

This week though, we were back to Darren. I knew I would have to tell them at some point but I still felt it was too soon. Dr. John felt otherwise. I already wasn't having a good day because the nurse wasn't allowed to leave my room until I ate all of my breakfast. My meals weren't big because of how small I was when I was admitted, and because my stomach was so small. Even half of a banana made me feel like a balloon. Now Dr. John wanted me to tell him about Darren?

I started to cry harder as I thought about him and the bad start to my day. I did not want to do this. I wanted to go back to my room. *No,* I wanted to go back home and be on my treadmill. That's where I wanted to be. Not here. Not with Dr. John.

Dr. John could tell I wasn't going to stop crying any time soon so instead of pressing me about Darren further, he let me cry. I sobbed and sobbed until I could barely breathe, and could feel a headache coming on. I must have cried for the rest of our session, but when finally looked up at Dr. John, he was still sitting at his desk, papers still strewn about.

"Aren't we- Aren't we done?" I asked. My voice was still shaky.

He shook his head, "No, Emily, not today. My client after you has asked to reschedule their appointment, which means I am free for the rest of the day. So we have all the time we want to talk about anything you want."

I laughed. "You mean we're going to talk about what you want to talk about? You've been pressing me about Darren since his named slipped my mouth two weeks ago." I snapped.

"Emily, while I am interested and do need to know what happened with Darren, I am more concerned about what you want to talk about. You're my client and I am here to help you."

"You don't have to tell me the whole story today. You could tell me bits and pieces, or just facts about Darren. But yes, I do want to talk about him, but not until you're ready to." Dr. John said firmly.

I didn't say anything; I just looked into his soft, green eyes. I felt bad for snapping at him. He was only trying to help me. But did I even want his help? What did I help for?

"Can I tell you about my first encounter with Darren?" I asked Dr. John.

"Certainly."

I took a deep breath and plunged head first into my story.

One, two, three. One, two, three. The count to our dance steps always got stuck in my head after a class. I was surprised at how well the class went given we have a new instructor now. Our old instructor, Ms. Barnes suffered a hip injury and needed a replacement, making her unavailable for the rest of our season. Our new instructor was a man named Darren. All of the girls, including me, loved Darren right from the start. He was a refreshing change to old, bitter Ms. Barnes. For example, we could just call him Darren. No prefix needed.

He asked us to introduce ourselves to him by doing a small dance routine individually so he could also get our sense of style that we put into the moves. Then he talked about his history with dance and how much he looked forward to working with us. He was a tall, tanned, muscular man. His eyes were a dark shade of blue, and he could work the facial hair. I think every girl found him and his jet black hair attractive.

The first class with Darren was fun; he taught us how to relax more and add in our little twist to the moves, the exact opposite to what Ms. Barnes had taught us.

"You may be dancing as a group, but the moves need individuality from each of you. Stiff boards are not attractive! Have fun with the moves and feel them!" He yelled over the music. It wasn't hard to feel the music; it flowed past your skin right down to your bones.

It was as if you could feel the beat of your music beating against your skin. It was exhilarating. This is what I loved about dance class.

In no time at all, class was over and we were back in the locker room packing away our things. I just finished brushing my now matted brown hair when Darren came over to me and asked if I could step into his office.

"Sure" I said and followed him to his office.

He sat down at his desk and told me to sit; I did as I was told. He didn't say anything at first, he just stared at me. I couldn't tell if I was in trouble or not, his eyes were unreadable. Say something, damn it. I thought.

"Emily, you are an excellent dancer. Did you know that?" He spoke softly, making sure I was listening.

I felt a blush creep up my neck. "Thank you, Darren. I practice very hard at home."

"Well it shows," he replied with a smile. "However, I have one little concern."

I looked at him anxiously. Was my timing off from everyone else? Was I too stiff? I didn't know what to say so I waited for him to continue.

"Your weight, Emily. I noticed you're a bit bigger than the other girls." He said.

I blinked at him. "My...my weight?" I started to panic. Was I really that fat? I had always been self-conscious, but I didn't think it was that bad.

"Yes, your weight." He said with a trace of annoyance in his voice. He stood up, and motioned for me to do the same. I stood.

He then walked to the office door, and shut it. My heart rate was picking up. Ms. Barnes never closed her office door unless she was leaving for the night.

"Come over to the mirror, Emily." He said softly.

I slowly walked over, wondering what was going to happen next. I now stood facing the mirror and Darren was close behind me, very close behind me. I could feel his breath on the back of my neck. Lift up your shirt to show your stomach. I did as I was told.

"See the fat here?" he asked. I nodded. "Lose it."

He then proceeded to point out I did not have a gap between my thighs like the other girls. I had more arm fat than the other girls. My collar bones didn't stick out as much as the other girls. I had back fat; I didn't even know that was possible. Darren pointed out

*all of the areas of my body that had fat and told me I needed to start working out
regularly if I wanted to lose the weight.*

*He turned me around to face him, his face now inches from mine. I wanted to lose this
weight. I wanted to lose it now. I wanted Darren to be happy with me, and right now he
wasn't. I wanted Darren to like me best, but he wouldn't until I was skinny. I needed to
be skinny now, for Darren.*

*"Emily, I wish you were beautiful like the other girls, but you are not thin like they are."
He said sadly. I'll lose it, I'll lose all the weight, Darren, don't worry. I thought.*

*Darren touched my face lightly and then turned away from me. "I'll lose the weight,
Darren. I can do it." I said proudly.*

*He turned to face me again, and smiled. "Good girl." We stood there for a moment
longer. "Lose at least 5 pounds by next week, we'll check back in at the end of class, and
if you have lost the weight, I will reward you. You must not tell the other girls this,
though, it will make them jealous." He said darkly.*

I smiled. I liked special treatment. "Okay." I said with a grin.

"Leave." Darren said, and again, I did as I was told.

*I couldn't wait to get home and lose this weight. I was going to make Darren proud, even
if it killed me.*

I was proud of myself for not crying while talking about Darren. I think Dr. John was
proud of me too because he was smiling at me. "You did wonderfully, Emily, thank you.
I think you can go back to your room for the day."

"We're not going to talk about it? Isn't this the part where you drill me with a million
questions about my story?" I asked, utterly confused.

Dr. John smiled at me then said, "No, not today. I think you need to ponder that memory
Emily. Sometimes you will find that I may give you "homework assignments." This just
means I want you to think about something for our next session. Well your very first
homework assignment is thinking about why Darren's opinion meant so much to you."

He packed up his things, and held out his arm to me. I was still weak, and I couldn't
always make it back to my room by myself. Dr. John has been escorting me after our
sessions. I didn't protest his request. I stood up and tucked my arm around his, and we
walked out of his office together.

When I got back to my room I was told dinner would be here shortly. Tonight's meal: a
chocolate pudding cup. I felt my heart rate start to rise, and my pulse was quickening.
Chocolate. Pudding. Chocolate. I couldn't eat something chocolate! That's so unhealthy!

I had to find a way to get out of eating this. I would definitely gain weight from this pudding cup and that could not happen. I tried watching T.V. to distract me but it wasn't working. I kept thinking about the pudding. The beeping from my heart monitor was annoying me, my anxiety was shooting through the roof and my cup full of fat would be here any minute. I didn't know what to do. The nurse had orders to stay here until I finished eating, so there was no way I could hide the pudding. I was doomed.

My pudding was brought to me, and at first I stared at it. I slowly picked up the spoon, and started to pull back the foil lid when a loud beeping noise came from the corner of my room, where the nurse was standing.

"Oh, no!" she exclaimed. She looked at me, "Emily, I have an emergency to tend to down the hall, I will be back as soon as I can. If you hide that pudding, I shall know." She ran from the room shouting "I'm coming!"

Yes! Now was my chance! I thought. I opened one of the drawers of my little bed side dresser, and scraped the contents of the cup into the drawer. I looked at the empty cup, pleased; it looked like I had eaten the pudding. For good measure, and with great difficulty, I licked the spoon, leaving little chocolate remnants on my tongue. *Good job, Darren would be proud.*

It was easier to focus on TV after I avoided eating the pudding, and before I knew it the nurse was back.

"Okay, Emily, let me see the pudding cup." She said sternly. I picked up the cup and the spoon, so she could see that I "ate it". She gave me a suspicious look then said "Open your mouth."

I did as I was told and even stuck out my tongue so she could see the chocolate on it. She nodded and gave me a look of approval. "Very good, Emily! That wasn't so hard was it?"

I glared at her. "It was terrifying." I said pretty convincingly.

She sighed. "Emily, eventually you will get better and you won't see the harm in eating a pudding cup." She took her place back in the chair in the corner. I had to have a nurse in here at all times, in case something went wrong. Sometimes it was annoying and other times it wasn't so bad. It depended on who my nurse was. The nurse I had now, made having her around all the time, unbearable. She treated me like a child, and I was not a child, I was eighteen years old.

My hospital phone rang, and I dreaded answering because I knew it would be my mother. "Hello?" I said as I picked up the receiver.

"Emily!" It wasn't my mother's voice, it was my friend Leah's voice, from gymnastics. She was one of the few good friends I had.

"Leah?!" I exclaimed. "How did you know I was in the hospital?"

"Your mom had to explain to Sarah (our gymnastics coach) why you would be gone for a while, and Sarah felt we had the right to know. I knew something was going on with you, you were dropping so much weight so fast! Are you okay?" she said this all very fast. That was Leah though. I missed her.

"I don't really know, Leah. I mean I think I'm okay, but the doctors don't. I like how I look by the way." Maybe it wasn't a good thing that Leah had called.

"Emily…I…I hope you get better…" she said quietly and quickly before hanging up the phone.

I looked at the receiver, slightly angry at Leah. I wasn't sick! There was nothing wrong with me! I was finally at my goal weight and everybody is treating that like it's a bad thing. I'm finally skinny. I wish I could- a light bulb went off in my head.

I told the nurse I needed to talk to my mom and asked if I could have 10 minutes of privacy for the call. She agreed but only because she needed to grab a quick bite to eat, and use the bathroom. As soon as she left the room, I dialed Darren's cell phone number.

It rang three times before he picked up. "Hello?" Oh, how I've missed his voice.

"Darren? It's Emily…" I said happily.

"Emily! How are you, love?" he asked excitedly.

"I'm finally under 90 pounds, Darren. No one else is happy for me though. They all want me to gain weight. I like being skinny." I whined to him.

He laughed. I could feel him smile on the other end. "You are finally beautiful, baby. I'm so proud of you. You don't have to eat anything they give you honey. You'll find ways to avoid it, I know you."

He made me feel so good about myself. "I miss you." I said sadly.

"Oh Em, don't be sad. I miss you too. I miss rewarding you, and I miss your dancing, but you'll be back soon enough." He said with a trace of sadness in his voice too.

"I have to go, the nurse is coming back." I said.

"Okay Emily, but remember, stay beautiful." He said sternly, and then hung up. I smiled. *I will, Darren, just for you.*

The nurse was back and she once again found her chair. I spent the rest of my night watching TV, until it was time for the nurse to do my nightly check up. Everything

looked good according to her, and it was lights out for me. Darren's dark blue eyes were the last thing I saw before I drifted off to sleep. *Stay Beautiful.*

As the week wore on, I grew to be disappointed with myself. I only managed to get out of eating my meals four more times. Every time I ate, I could feel the food sit in my stomach and it made me feel disgusting. I wanted it out of me. Sometimes, I would turn on the shower while I was going to the bathroom, and I would throw up my meal. The nurses haven't found out yet. I knew Darren wouldn't be pleased if he knew either, well he'd be proud about the throwing up but not about the times I've eaten the food. I wasn't looking forward to my next session with Dr. John either because I knew he would ask me about Darren again.

Tuesday morning came quicker than I anticipated, and I was given my breakfast as usual. A granola bar and some yogurt. I ate it with disgust, and felt my stomach getting heavier and heavier. Did they want me to look like I was pregnant? One o'clock was drawing nearer and nearer. Finally, at 12:30 I told the nurse I was too sick to go see Dr. John today. She retorted with "That's okay; Dr. John said he would be glad to come here for your session any time you can't make it to his office."

I frowned and said "Never mind, I'll go". At least our appointments got me out of my room for two hours. My nurse escorted me down to Dr. John's office, and I was glad to leave her. I think her diet consisted only of cabbage because she always smelled of it.

I walked into Dr. John's office and took my usual spot on the couch. The room felt hotter than usual, and it seemed smaller to me. Normally I found the soft, dark blue walls comforting, but this time, all I could think was *Darren.* The ticking of the clock seemed louder than usual too.

"Emily" Dr. John's voice called me back from my thoughts. "I have quite a few things to discuss with you today." His voice was quiet, and stern. He clearly was not happy today.

"Okay…" I said. "Dr. John, you seem mad today. Are you?" I asked hesitantly.

He closed his eyes and sighed. He opened his eyes again and I knew the answer was yes. "Yes, Emily, I am mad. You will find out why if you let me continue speaking. You will not interrupt me until I am finished speaking, is that understood?" This did not seem like a question, but a command.

I nodded, I was too afraid to speak right now.

"Firstly," he started flipping through some papers. "You have managed to avoid eating some of your meals, including dumping a pudding cup in your dresser drawer."

I bowed my head. I thought I had gotten away with that.

"Secondly, you have thrown up some of your meals." He said sternly, though he didn't look at me yet.

I still didn't say anything, I knew he wasn't finished.

"And thirdly, you got in contact with Darren." He said trying to hide his anger.

I looked up and opened my mouth is protest, but Dr. John held up his hand.

"Save the lies, Emily. Let me explain something to you. You are sick. Very sick. I am here to help you. Now I understand that you are sick, and I do not expect you to get better right away, but I expect you to give effort. I know you can get better, Emily. I want you to get better, as do your mother and friends. The food infractions are somewhat understandable seeing your condition. However, contacting Darren was completely out of line. Surely you knew that. He is the reason you are here, Emily. We both know that after last week's session. I am here to help you, as are the nurses and doctor's but we need to see effort from you. You want to go home, and get back to dance and gymnastics, that will not happen unless you eat. Do you understand me, Emily?"

I sat there for a moment, taking in his words. I still didn't believe I was sick. I liked being skinny, it was beautiful. I did want to go home though, and I didn't want Dr. John to be mad at me, he was the only one I somewhat liked in the hospital.

"I can try to try Dr. John. I still don't think I'm sick though. I like being this skinny." I said firmly.

"I know, Emily. That's why you come to see me. But I must warn you, talking to Darren will not get you home sooner, and if you do it again, there will be consequences, understood?"

"Yes, I understand." I grumbled. "What are we talking about today?" Eager to change the subject.

"Well, why don't we talk about your week? You've managed to throw away food, and throw up food, so let's talk about that." He said lightly.

So we did. I told him how the food feels in my stomach, and how I'm scared I will instantly gain weight if I eat it. I told him it was easy to skip meals before I came here. I grew to hate food.

Finally we reached the last fifteen minutes of our session. "Emily, if you remember, I gave you a homework assignment last week. Do you remember what that is?"

"You asked me to think about why Darren's opinion matters so much to me." I said quietly.

"And did you come up with anything?" He asked.

I didn't answer right away. Then finally I said, "No, I didn't. I, uh, actually forgot about it. I didn't think much about it after I talked to Darren that night. I was too focused on not eating."

Dr. John let out a heavy sigh. He does that a lot I noticed. "Emily, this will again be your homework assignment, until you come up with something. I suggest you put more thought into it." It wasn't a suggestion though, it was a command. Dr. John wouldn't take my bullshit, I could tell.

Our two hours were up and Dr. John escorted me back to my room, like usual. I had a lot to think about.

I didn't bother turning on the TV. I had so much going through my mind that I actually wanted to sit down and think to try and calm the noise in my head. I felt pretty lousy after my session with Dr. John and I knew in some ways he was right.

I want to go home, more than anything. I don't want to be here anymore, but if I keep rebelling they'll keep me here even longer. I can't stand to eat and not work out though. I'll be able to feel the food sitting inside me. Suddenly, an idea came to me. I picked up my phone and called Dr. John. He had given me his number after our first session in case I ever needed him. He picked up on the second ring.

"Hello?" he said briskly.

"Dr. John, it's Emily."

"Oh, Emily! Is everything alright? Our session just ended…" he sounded confused.

"I'm fine, I have a question for you though. I've been thinking about what you said. About how I need to eat, and put in effort or else I won't go home soon."

"Mmhmm, go on."

"Well, I'll feel disgusting if I eat and then just sit around all day. Would it be okay if I took a walk after my meals? Not a really long one, just around the floor a couple of times." I pleaded.

He paused, and I could tell he was actually considering my proposal. "Well, I don't see why not. For now, you may take a walk after every meal. The nurse will be with you, and when she says your walk is over, you are to go back to your room without protest do you understand?"

Joy spread through out my body. He actually said yes! "Oh yes! Thank you Dr. John, thank you!"

He laughed. "You're welcome, Emily."

The days were more tolerable with my walks after every meal. I was so happy Dr. John let me do this. The nurse and I usually walked around the floor fifteen times before heading back to my room, I didn't feel so bad about eating most days.

I hadn't heard from Leah and I wasn't sure if I was upset or glad that she hadn't tried calling me either. I was upset that I couldn't talk to Darren though. I missed him. I knew that if I kept eating, and going for my walks, I would soon be allowed to go home, back to Darren and back to dance.

My mom called that night and I told her about my walks, she was just glad to hear I was actually eating. She still feels terrible that she didn't notice my weight, but I'm glad that she didn't. She said she wishes she could visit me, but I'm not allowed visitors yet. I don't quite know why, but I'm glad I'm not because my mom would be here every day if she could. She would eventually drive me insane.

My meals were also getting slightly bigger, and I was starting to regain my strength. I still needed an escort though. It was a scary day when the doctor came in and said they needed to check my weight. I hadn't checked my weight in so long, and I didn't want to see the number. I was sure it would cause me to panic and I wouldn't even want to eat.

Dr. Mills came in, accompanied by Dr. John. He was my moral support I assumed. They helped me out of bed and into the bathroom. I stared at the scale and started to tear up.

"I can't do this" I whimpered. Dr. John sat me down in a chair and knelt down in front of me.

"Emily, you *can* do this. That number on the scale does not make you beautiful. We need you healthy, and that means the number needs to go up." He said calmly, not taking his eyes off of mine.

"Okay," I said. "I'll do it."

"Good girl." Said Dr. Mills.

I closed my eyes and they guided me on the scale. After a second, I heard a small gasp. I opened my eyes and looked down at the scale. *85 lbs.* I let out a sigh of relief. I didn't gain weight! If only I could tell Darren! I looked up at Dr. Mills and Dr. John. They were looking at each other, deciding what to do.

"Emily, Dr. John and I have something to discuss, then I might have some phone calls to make, and then we'll be back to discuss this." Dr. Mills said flatly before he and Dr. John left my room. I knew they weren't happy about my weight loss but I couldn't be happier.

Although, I don't know how I managed to regain strength and lose weight at the same time. I didn't question it too much though. I was just glad I wasn't over 90 pounds again. Today was going to be better than I thought it would be! I was in a good mood and nothing could bring me down!

...

Wrong. Dr. Mills and Dr. John came back later to give me news that brought me out of my good mood completely. They weren't at all happy about my weight loss, and after throwing away food and throwing up food, they couldn't trust me to eat by myself, even with a nurse in the room. I was allowed one walk a day, and from now, I would be fed through a tube until my weight was back up. I cried and I pleaded, but they had made up their minds.

'Emily, do you realize what is going to happen to you if you don't start eating?" Dr. Mills asked, but I barely heard him. His voice was growing fainter, and the room was closing in on itself.

"Emily!"

"Emily!"

Everyone was shouting my name, but I couldn't answer them, the world was slipping away from me and I couldn't stop it. I couldn't see, couldn't hear, and couldn't feel. I was gone.

Chapter 2

woke up to a plethora of voices and beeping. I knew I must still be in the hospital. I could hear Dr. Mills somewhere in the room, talking to an unfamiliar voice. I tried opening my eyes, but it was very difficult. I let them stay closed for a little while longer.

The second time I woke up, it was much easier to open my eyes. The lights were so bright that I had to squint. My whole body felt strange, heavier, I didn't like it. The beeping noises from all the monitors were still there and I had wires and tubes all over me. I went to talk but found that I couldn't because of a tube down my throat. There was no one in the room except for….but no…it couldn't be….Dr. John wouldn't let him….Darren?

It was him alright; the tanned skin, jet black hair, and those sparkling dark blue eyes. I was so happy I could cry! I couldn't believe he was really here! To see me! Darren got up out of the chair and strode over to my bed, where he bent down and whispered "Emily".

"Emily."

"Emily."

I opened my eyes, my heart sinking immediately. Darren wasn't actually here. It had been a dream. I felt foolish for believing he would actually be here. Instead it was Dr. Mills who was standing over me. I never knew how old he really was until now; you could see little creases in his face. I went to speak, but I still couldn't because of the tube in my throat. Of course that part of the dream would be true.

"Emily, you gave everyone quite a scare." Dr. Mills said softly. All I could do was look at him. "You went into cardiac arrest."

My eyes spoke the shock I was feeling. *Died? I almost died?* Tears stung my eyes and started rolling down my cheeks. I didn't want to die; I just wanted to be beautiful for Darren. Maybe I did need to eat just a bit more. I couldn't be beautiful for Darren if I were dead. I wasn't sure how I was going to go about fixing this. I couldn't eat because then I would be fat, and not beautiful. If I continue to not eat, I'm going to die, and then I'll have no chance of being beautiful. I should just wait until I have my next session with Dr. John and see what he says. Yes, that's a good idea.

Dr. Mills went on to explain that I would be staying here until I was in stable condition, and the rest of my treatment would be discussed once I was stable. I still wasn't allowed any visitors. I just wanted to see my mom, surprisingly. She would be comforting and helping to take care of me. I knew I had to deal with this though, I didn't have a choice.

It was a week before I was stable and didn't have a tube down my throat anymore. I learned that it had been a feeding tube. I was so scared to see how much I weighed, but then I just reminded myself that if I didn't gain at least a little bit of weight, I would die. My whole body was sore and felt foreign, but I guess that's what happens when you don't get much use out of it for a whole week, even longer actually, I had been unconscious for three days before Dr. Mills told me what had happened.

They let my mom visit but only because she wouldn't stop calling the hospital and bugging to speak to Dr. Mills. Apparently they argued several times about visiting me, and eventually Dr. Mills gave in once my condition was stable.

I was really happy to see her. She greeted me with a big, but fragile hug, since I was still under weight. She also bought me a teddy bear from the gift shop. It was cute, I guess. She didn't talk about my issues much; she was mainly filling me in on her drama from work and around the neighborhood back at home. I learned to tune her out when she does this, and I swear she almost never notices. The only problem with this is it leads me thinking about my dad.

He left my mom and me when I was two, and mom still won't tell me why he left. Every time I ask her about it, she changes the subject or says "It doesn't matter". I disagree. It does matter, at least to me. I want to know why he didn't want to stay, and I was going to ask again.

"Mom" I interrupted some story about work, but I didn't care.

She sighed, "Yes, Emily?"

"Tell me why Dad left." I said quietly, looking straight into her gray eyes. They looked scared.

She sighed again, "Well I can tell you weren't listening to my story. I've told you plenty of times Emily, it doesn't matter. He left, and it's his loss. The important thing is we have each other." She lightly brushed back a strand of my hair and leaned in to kiss my cheek.

I'm not sure how, but this small gesture brought on tears that I didn't realize I had been holding back. It started out with a small, choked sob, and my mom wrapped her arms around me. I sat in her lap, with her arms wrapped around me for quite a while. Her shirt was soft, and smelled like lavender. It was comforting. I never realized how much I missed my mom until now. I could stay like this forever. Her hand was rubbing my back, and she was making "shh" noises. My sobs were beginning to slow, and my nose was running. My mom's shoulder was now covered in my tears and snot. I sat up and looked at her. She was wearing a soft expression full of worry, and love. Oh, mom.

"Are you okay now, baby doll?" She asked quietly. I nodded. I felt slightly better, truthfully; almost as if a small weight had been lifted. "Let's get you back to your room, okay?" Again, I nodded. I grabbed my new teddy bear and my mother's hand, and we began the walk back to my room.

…

I woke up the next morning feeling slightly groggy, and confused. The memories of the day before slowly started coming back to me. My mom's visit, my breakdown, and my new teddy bear. I wonder if the doctors would still let her visit after what happened. I got up and went into my bathroom and took a quick shower.

The warm water hitting my skin felt absolutely wonderful; I was getting goose bumps. I let the water run over my skin and ran my hands through my hair. This felt so refreshing! I felt my stress spinning down the drain with the water, and the smell of my apple body wash was filling the air. I think today will be a good day.

Not long after I got out of the shower, a nurse came to tell me that I had an appointment with Dr. John in half an hour. Normally, I would be annoyed, but today, I don't mind so much. I continued getting dressed and sat combing my hair on the edge of my bed. Maybe I would be willing to talk more about Darren today, maybe.

I took my familiar place on the leather couch, and greeted Dr. John with a cheery "hello".

"You seem to be in a good mood today." Dr. John said with a smile.

"Yeah, I just have a feeling that today will be a good day." I said, returning the smile.

"Well, let's hope this session doesn't spoil that for you. Why don't you tell me what put you in such a good mood?" he replied.

"Has anyone ever told you that crying makes you feel better?" I asked.

"Yes, plenty of times."

"Well, my mom visited yesterday, and we were talking about…stuff, and I started crying. Really hard. She held me while I cried. She bought me a teddy bear from the gift shop. Today I just feel better after crying so much yesterday."

Dr. John nodded and paused before answering, gathering his thoughts. "Why were you crying yesterday, Emily?"

"I think…I really felt the weight of everything that's happened to me in the past couple of weeks, and I didn't know I was holding so much in until the tears started flowing."

"I'm glad you mentioned that, because that's something we need to talk about today. But first, why don't you tell me what you and your mom were talking about that triggered you crying."

I sighed. This was the only thing that I didn't want to talk about. "I don't really want to talk about it…"

"Well what would you like to talk about, Emily?"

I shrugged. "I dunno." I said softly. The tears started coming again. *What the hell is wrong with me?!* I wasn't sobbing this time, it was a silent cry. The tears just flowed down my cheeks but I didn't make a sound. I could feel Dr. John watching me. I sniffled and wiped my nose on the edge of my sleeve. "We were talking about my dad…" I said after a couple of minutes.

"What specifically about your dad?" he asked.

I took in a deep breath, and focused on my hands in my lap. "He left my mom and me when I was two. I still don't know why he did, and mom won't tell me why. Yesterday, I asked her again and she still didn't tell me, and I just started crying."

"Emily, sometimes things are better left unsaid. It may frustrate you that your mom won't tell you the truth about your dad, but there's probably a very good reason for that."

"And what reason would that be?"

"She loves you and wants to protect you."

"I just want to know why he left me…why wasn't I good enough?" I asked, my voice sounding desperate.

"You *are* good enough. Your dad is missing out on a wonderful, young lady. Your dad is part of your past, and he needs to stay there. You need to start focusing on the future, Emily." Said Dr. John.

I nodded. Dr. John was right. I shouldn't focus on something that I couldn't fix, let alone find the truth about.

"Emily, do you think that your father's absence has something to do with Darren?" he asked quietly and cautiously.

I looked up at him, and just blinked. "Actually, no…I-I've never thought about that."

"Well how about we think about this together?" he asked.

"Darren made me feel special…" I said.

"How did he make you feel special, Emily?"

The next week I arrived to dance practice early, eager to show Darren I had lost the weight. I lost more than he asked me to. He would be so happy. I walked to Darren's office door and knocked. A few seconds later, Darren appeared. His face spread into a smile. "Emily, come in." He gestured for me to sit.

I didn't sit though. I walked over to the mirror because I knew we would end up there. He followed me over, and looked at me in the mirror. Our eyes found one another, and he was smirking at me.

"Lift up your shirt first." I did and he inspected my stomach by pinching it lightly, nodding in approval. He looked at my arms, and was still pleased. A tiny gap was forming between my thighs, and my collarbones were slightly more visible. He told me I could pull my shirt back down.

"Step on the scale." He said as he pulled out a scale from the closet. I stepped on, and watched the number change until it finally stopped on 120. He nodded.

"Seven pounds less than last week, Emily. Good job." He said softly, his eyes glistening in the dim lighting of the office. His eyes were so beautiful.

I stepped off the scale, and stood inches from Darren. He stepped towards me. "I worked really hard to lose the weight." I said proudly. Darren smiled again. "I can tell. You are a very hard worker Emily. I like that about you. Now, I believe I told you last week I would reward you if you lost the weight." He said with a playful smile. What did he mean? What was he going to do?

He stepped towards me again until our bodies were almost touching and he looked down at me, his eyes smoldering. I could feel his breathing increasing, and I could feel my heart start to race. He slowly lifted his hand to my cheek, and brushed back a piece of my hair. Was he going to do what I thought he was going to do? His face started moving closer to mine. Oh my...he was! My stomach was doing backflips, and I felt my heart in my throat. Before I knew it, Darren's soft, warm lips were on mine, but just briefly. My mind exploded with fireworks, and his body felt glorious pressed slightly against mine. His hand felt soft against my cheek, and I wished we could stay like that forever.

He pulled back, and smiled. "How did you like your reward?"

I giggled, and felt a blush spread to my cheeks. "I liked it..." I said quietly.

"Good," he pulled me to him. "Continue your hard work, Emily. Maybe you'll get more rewards." He winked, and turned away from me. He opened the door, and motioned that it was time for me to leave.

I don't know why but I couldn't look him in the eyes as I walked out of his office. All I could think about was the way his lips felt against mine.

I couldn't look Dr. John in the eye for most of my story. I knew he wouldn't approve of what had happened. He sighed a deep, heavy sigh. "Well, Emily, something will have to be done about Darren, I hope you know that."

My body filled with dread, and the color drained from my face. "What? N-no…no…I'm eighteen, I'm legal, it's okay…" I stammered.

"You were still a minor at the time, Emily. I have to do something about this." He said sternly.

A fresh round of tears started streaming down my face, and I couldn't control the sobs that followed. Darren couldn't get in trouble…this would ruin everything.

"Please Dr. John…don't do anything. He'll know I've told and I promised him I wouldn't. Please. I'm okay.." He held up his hand, telling me to stop talking.

"Emily, we both know that you are not okay, and I have to do something about this, it's part of my job. Why would you promise something like that?" he asked, tilting his head to the side.

I was still crying, but my sobs were controlled now. "Because….because I love him."

"Emily, I wish we had the time to talk about your feelings for Darren, but our session is almost over, and I have something important to tell you." He said calmly.

I sniffled. "Okay."

"Dr. Mills and I have discussed this since you had that heart attack. We have also discussed this with your mother, and she agrees. We are going to be sending you to a mental hospital for more intense treatment." He said heavily.

Wait…what? A *mental hospital?* No, I don't belong there! I'm…I'm fine, I don't need to go. No.

"Why?! I don't need to go there. I need to go home!" I shouted. I was starting to shake and I could feel my face was getting hot. This was not going to happen!

Dr. John waited for me to finish shouting before saying, "Emily, you do need further treatment. Sessions with me won't be enough, and the attention you need cannot be provided at a regular hospital. You are sick, mentally. You need the help. Also, you don't have a choice. You need to pack your things because you're leaving in a couple of hours."

I glared at him. This was not fair! I crossed my arms over my chest and turned away from him. I knew I was acting childish but I didn't care right now. I didn't want to go to a mental hospital! No, scratch that. I don't *need* to go to a mental hospital. I'm fine. Maybe they couldn't stop me from going, but I could resist the help once I was there.

"Emily?" Dr. John asked. "You really should go back to your room and start packing up your things. You're leaving soon, as I've said."

I sighed. "Fine." I said angrily, and stormed out of his office. Since I had to force fed through that feeding tube when I nearly died, I put enough weight back on that gave me enough strength to actually walk without an escort. I was so thankful for that at this moment. I did not want to be with Dr. John a second longer.

I slammed the door to my room, not caring how many residents I disturbed. The phone rang and I reached to pick up it.

"Hello?" I said not bothering to hide the agitation in my voice.

"Emily? Sweetie?" My mom's voice came in fuzzy and far away.

I rolled my eyes and hung up the phone. I started grabbing my clothes from my dresser drawers and stuffing them in my suitcase. I didn't like being in the hospital, but I didn't want to go to another kind of hospital either.

A knock came from my door and I glanced at it, debating whether to answer it or not. I realized I didn't have much of a choice, this wasn't actually my room. I walked over and opened the door and it was Dr. Mills and Dr. John. Great. I glared at both of them before saying "What do you want?"

They looked at each other and didn't say anything at first. They walked into my room and Dr. Mills asked me to sit down.

"Emily, we don't want you to be angry with us. This is to help you. You're one step closer to going home." Dr. Mills said calmly.

"You'll still be seeing me Emily. I will be your therapist while you're there. I should also warn you, resisting treatment will keep you from going home." He said raising an eyebrow at me.

My heart sank. I didn't want to see Dr. John anymore, and now I had no choice but to go through with treatment. I could still be angry at them though. They couldn't stop me from being angry.

"Dr. John if you don't mind, I'd like to have a word with Emily." Dr. Mills said, looking me dead in the eye.

Dr. John nodded, and placed a hand on my shoulder before leaving my room. Was it just me or was my room really warm today? The curtains were opened wide, and sunlight was streaming in. Oh, well that's why. My room always smelled strongly of disinfectant and some other smell I couldn't place. I sat criss-crossed on my bed, and waited for Dr. Mills to start speaking.

"Emily, in a way, it has been a joy to be your doctor over the past couple of weeks." He said.

"What?" I said, slightly taken aback.

"I can tell that you're starting to get better, very slowly, but you are. You are such a lovely young woman, and I will always hope the best for you. I just want you to promise me one thing." He said sternly.

"And what is that?" I asked somewhat sarcastically.

"Promise me that you will try to get better while you are there, that you won't resist treatment." He practically pleaded.

I just looked at him. My first reaction was to reject him, tell him that I would refuse treatment until they gave up on me and sent me home. But I couldn't tell him that. This man saved my life more than once, I wouldn't be here right now if it weren't for him. I decided I owed him this much.

"Dr. Mills, I still don't agree that I need treatment, but I promise as long as I'm there I won't resist treatment." I said.

He smiled, and relief flooded his face. "I know you can recover, Emily. You just have to work towards it." He squeezed my hand before leaving my room. Dr. John came back in and told me he would be riding with me to this hospital. I looked at him, confused.

"What about my mom?" I asked.

"Well, since you hung up on her when she tried calling, she decided she would just visit you on your first visitors day. It'll give you time to cool off." He said coolly. I could tell he wasn't pleased with how I treated my mom, but I didn't really care. "Are all of your things packed? We still have to check you out."

"Yes." I said softly. I looked around my hospital room. This had become my home over the past couple of weeks. I nearly died here, twice. I hid food in here. I spent hours crying into my pillows, curled up in ball under my sheets. The white board on the wall had "Nancy" written in loopy, pink writing. She was my nurse for the past three days. I walked over the window and looked out on the busy streets of New York. Cars and buses were passing by, filled with people moving on with their lives. Traveling to work, or school or to visit family and friends. Here I was, about to move into a mental hospital, because I wasn't like those people in the cars and buses. I couldn't go home. I couldn't go to school. I wasn't like them and I don't think I ever will be. This realization hit me hard, and tears filled my eyes. I sniffled, and wiped my nose with my sleeve. I turned to face Dr. John and saw that he was only standing inches from me. I let out a sob and he pulled me close to him. I sobbed into his jacket, and he pet my hair. We stood like this for a while, before he pulled back and whispered "We have to go." I nodded and picked up my suitcase. He nudged me forward, and together we walked out of my room. I stopped in the door way and I looked back one more time. I closed my eyes and let out a deep breath. *I can only go up from here.* I thought.

Chapter 3

The place was called "Reach for the Stars." I already didn't want to be here but I remembered my promise to Dr. Mills and tried to find something positive about this place. The lady at the check in desk was overly nice, and bubbly. She annoyed me. She had rosy cheeks, that had nothing to do with blush, and big brown eyes that seemed to be watery all the time. Her hair was gray and short, but it complimented her round face nicely. She was a big woman, but short. She gave a sheet of paper that had my "schedule" on it. I don't even know if schedule was the right word for it.

had one-on-one therapy sessions with Dr. John three times a week; Monday, Wednesday, and Friday. 2:00 pm to 3:00 pm.

Group Therapy was twice a week: Tuesday and Thursday. 5:00 pm to 7:00 pm.

was supposed to take art classes on Saturdays from 11:00 am until noon.

Sundays were visitors' day.

Breakfast was at 9:00 am, lunch was at 12:00 pm and dinner was at 7:00 pm. I stared at this part of my schedule the most. I wondered if I was going to be forced to eat all three meals. I hoped not. I couldn't do that.

Dr. John thanked the check-in lady; I learned her name was Ms. Ruth. Dr. John told me he had to go to his office but my new roommate was going to show me to my room and help me get settled in. We had a therapy session later today; it was Monday.

"You're leaving me?" I said like a little girl whose mommy told her she was going to work.

He turned to look at me, "You'll see me in a couple of hours, Emily. You'll be okay." His voice was reassuring, and I couldn't help but believe him. I nodded and he turned, continuing towards his office.

A girl showed up a few seconds later. She had long, black hair and she was kind of short. She had faint freckles on her face, and her eyes were a pale green. She wore long sleeves and long pants, though I didn't blame her, it was chilly in the building. She looked friendly, and I hoped she turned out to be that way.

"Hi," she said in a soft voice. I wasn't sure if this was how her voice actually was, or if she was trying not to be loud. "I'm Gemma, I'm your roommate." She held out a hand to me, and smiled.

I took her hand and shook it. "I'm Emily. Nice to meet you." I said nervously.

"Let's go to our room." She said excitedly and practically pulled me down the hall.

On our way to our room I heard shrieks from girls doing God-knows-what, and shouts from boys who were probably playing video games or something. I had no idea what to expect of this place. I think they tried making the hallways fun and decorative, but it just looked tacky covered in paintings done by the other kids and motivational posters you normally see in classrooms at school. The tiles of the floor were confusing, they had these metallic dots embedded in them that made it look like you were walking on something that wasn't the ground. The walls, apart from the tacky paintings and posters, were white. White floors, white ceilings, white doors. I thought I had seen enough white back at the hospital to last me a lifetime, I was wrong apparently.

Gemma stopped outside of a room labeled 113A. This was my new room inside my new home, and I'm not sure how I feel about it. Gemma's side was already decorated in art she had made herself (which was not tacky like the ones in the hallway), hers were actually quite beautiful. They were mostly of nature. I could tell she liked trees. She had several paintings of trees in the summer, in the winter, in forests, on a beach. Each one was unique and exquisite, I couldn't help but stare. Her side of the room was also fairly messy. She had clothes strewn on the floor and on her bed, which she did not make. Her bed was covered in dark purple sheets and I saw a notebook sitting on the table next to

her bed. I knew nothing about this girl yet I somehow knew that that side of the room defined exactly who she was.

Gemma plopped down on her bed and said "So, there's not really much rules for decorating, so long as you don't permanently damage their property, you're good."

"Okay." I said timidly. I put my suitcase on my bed and began to unpack my clothes.

"Do you want me to help you unpack?" Gemma asked.

I turned and stared at her. I didn't expect her to help me. "Sure" I said and I couldn't help but smile.

She came over to my side of the room, and I told her just to shove all of my clothes into drawers, I didn't care where they went. It didn't take us long to unpack my clothes, since all I had was whatever was with me at the hospital. Gemma seemed to notice this too because she asked me about it.

"Dude, you have like nothing with you…"

I blushed. "I came from the hospital, so all I have with me right now is what I had there."

"Ohhhh," she said. "Well, don't worry, you'll have the chance to decorate it."

"Gemma, how long have you been here? If you don't mind me asking?" I said nervously.

She looked puzzled for a second, as if she couldn't remember. "Hmmm…almost a year?" she said as if it were no big deal.

I, however, stared at her in disbelief. "A- a year?"

"Yeah, but there are some people who have been here for about 2 years. Glad I'm not one of them." She said with a smile.

I was starting to panic. I couldn't be here that long! It was bad enough that I was already away from Darren for a couple of weeks! I had to get back home! Gemma had noticed that something was wrong because she was shaking me, pulling me away from my thoughts. Her hands were cold.

"Hey! Emily! What's wrong?" she sounded genuinely concerned.

"I can't be here that long…I need to be back home." I said with disbelief.

She laughed. "You're cute. And naïve. Nobody goes home quickly. You'll be here for at least a couple of months."

"I don't need to be here! I'm fine!" I almost shouted.

Gemma sat me down my bed. "Emily, right now, I'm afraid to hug you because I feel as though I'm going to break you, that's how skinny you are. You're fucked up, just like the rest of us. You need to accept that if you want to go home." She said flatly. She got up and grabbed my hand. "C'mon. You should meet some people before you're thrown into group."

She walked me down the hall to a large room filled with kids. The lighting was dim, and the walls were a tannish color, a break from the white. The floor was hardwood. It had a cozy feeling to it. I liked it. There was a T.V., some couches, a pool table, a bookshelf, and some board games. This was one of those rec room type things. There were two girls sitting in arm chairs facing each other and Gemma took me right to them.

"Leila, Anna, this is Emily. She's new. She just got here today, and she's my roommate." Gemma said politely.

One of the girls, a petite, blonde, stood and extended her arm. "I'm Leila." Her voice was strong and confident for someone who was in a mental hospital. She looked at me for a couple of seconds, and her mouth stretched into a smile. "You're like me."

"Huh?" I said. But a few seconds later I realized what she meant. She was really skinny, and pale, just like me. She didn't eat either. "Oh, yeah." Was all I could come up with.

Anna stood up next and extended her arm as well. She was average for a girl her height. Her eyes had fear in them though. I wasn't sure if it was because of me or if she was always like that. They were a light brown, almost copper. She had platinum blonde hair and was the first tall person I saw around here. "Hi Emily. It's nice to meet you." She said shyly. She sat right back down.

Gemma leaned into me, "Anna is somewhat new, only been here about a month or so. She'll warm up to you once she gets to know you."

I nodded. Gemma told Leila she was going to introduce me to more people, and Leila sat back down and resumed her conversation with Anna. Gemma walked me over to the pool table which was surrounded by guys.

"Hey!" Gemma yelled. All of the guys stopped and looked at us. "This here is Emily. Be nice to her or I'll kick all of your asses." She said sternly. I could tell she had power over the guys. It was understandable too, she was gorgeous.

One of the guys standing opposite of us, spoke up. He was tall, somewhat lanky, and had jet black hair. His eyes looked almost black from where we stood, and I noticed a tattoo on the inside of his wrist, though I couldn't tell exactly what it was from here. "Gem, relax. You always assume the worst from us."

"That's because when Alexis was here you tortured her for a week straight." She snarled.

"Alexis was a little bitch." The tattoo guy said. "Are you a bitch?" he looked at me.

"Uhm, I don't think so…" I said, quite frightened.

Gemma looked at me with a soft expression. "Emily is not a bitch." She said fiercely to the guys.

The tattoo guy smiled at me. "Well, then we have no reason to be mean to her." He walked over and said "I'm Caleb. It's very nice to meet you, Emily." His teeth were perfectly straight, and white. He was much taller than I and he was intimidating. I shook his hand only briefly before letting go. I wasn't sure how I felt about Caleb. The rest of the guys said hello and continued on with their game of pool. "Gemma, I think I can take over the rest of Emily's tour." He winked.

"Way to be subtle, Caleb. And no thanks, I got this." She said as she steered me out of the room. Truthfully, I was thankful Gemma stood her ground, I would have been uncomfortable with Caleb. Caleb, however, looked less than happy about Gemma's response. He looked like a lost puppy as we walked down the hall.

Gemma showed me the cafeteria, the courtyard, and green rooms were kids were allowed to smoke their cigarettes. She showed me a quieter lounge room, the nurse's office and the laundry room. She also showed me the art classroom, apparently almost everyone took art classes. Then she took me back to the main lobby, where the check-in lady was. There was a big display on the wall opposite, with everyone's name on it, and various numbers of gold stars next to them.

"This" she said "is the ruler of Reach for the Stars." She waved her arm in front of the display. I didn't realize how many people were here. There had to be at least 50 people.

"What?" I asked, confused and in awe at the same time.

"The number of stars you earn determines how much freedom you have around here. If you have one to five stars, you need to be escorted everywhere, you can't travel alone. If you have six to ten stars, you can travel to the rec room and art classroom alone, but that's it. If you have ten stars or above, you can travel alone. You have to earn the stars by going to your therapy sessions, not breaking the specific rules for your sickness. Always having good behavior, meaning no fighting, no defacing property, stuff like that. You have to have good behavior for two weeks straight though." She explained.

"That seems easy." I said, still staring at the board.

She laughed. "It seems it, but it's not. I can tell it's going to be hard for you." She said with a smirk.

I turned to her, "And why's that?" I growled.

She cocked her head to the side and said "Because you still don't think you're sick." She started to walk away, but remembered I couldn't be left alone so she waited for me to start following her and we walked back to our room in silence.

We each sat on our beds not saying anything until I thought of something I should have asked her when we first met.

"Gemma." I said softly.

"Hmm?" she had immersed herself in a magazine.

"Why are you here?" I asked nervously. I wasn't sure if the question would throw her into a fit of rage or make her breakdown in tears.

She looked up from her magazine and thought about how she was going to answer my question. "You'll find out eventually." She said flatly, and returned her to magazine.

"Why can't you tell me now?" I asked, slightly annoyed. She knew why I was here.

She looked at me again, and a small smile came across her face. I hate when she does that. "Tell you what. When you realize you're fucked up like the rest of us, then I'll tell you."

"What if you have to talk about it in group therapy?" I said with satisfaction.

She smirked, "We have group on different days. I won't be with you."

I turned away from her and realized, I may never know why she's here.

Two o'clock was almost here and I didn't quite know where Dr. John's office was so I figured I should leave around one fifty. I asked Gemma if she was my escort and she told me no, there would be someone here for me in a couple of minutes.

At almost one fifty five, five minutes later than I wanted to leave, I heard a knock on our half closed door. It was tattoo guy, I couldn't remember his name. *You've got to be kidding me.* I thought. I rolled my eyes as I told Gemma I'd see her later, and she gave me a sly smile as I walked out the door.

"Emily, right?" tattoo guy said.

"Yeah," I said playing with a loose thread on my shirt. "I'm sorry, I'm really bad with names so I don't remember yours."

He laughed. "It's okay. The first day is overwhelming anyway. Caleb."

I nodded. "So Emily, mind telling me why you're here?" I couldn't tell if he was trying to make small talk because he actually wanted to know or if because he just didn't want silence.

I sighed. "I don't need to be here. I have no reason to be." I said haughtily.

Caleb laughed again, harder this time. "There's a reason you're here. They don't send sane people here, much as that may surprise you. You've got a far way to Emily."

We stopped outside a door with Dr. John's name on it in shiny gold letters. "Here we are." Caleb said. "I'll be back at three to take you back to your room. Oh, and yes, I am your escort, unless I do something to ruin that." He smirked and walked away. *What is it with everyone smirking?* I thought. I pushed open the door and Dr. John already had my file out and a pen ready.

His office was similar to the one at the hospital. There were more chairs though. The walls were still a dark blue like his one at the hospital. There were tacky posters here though; I tried not to pay attention to them. I sat down on the biggest couch and curled up against the arm.

"Have you settled in okay, Emily?" Dr. John asked, piling papers into a neat stack.

"Yes. I don't have much like Gemma does." I said flatly. "My roommate." I added by his look of confusion.

"Well you didn't have much with you but I'm sure your mom would be happy to send you some of your things." He said.

I nodded absent mindedly. "Gemma won't tell me why she's here. She said I have to realize that I'm fucked up too, and then she'll tell me." I furrowed my brows together as I thought more about this. "Then Caleb told me they don't send sane people here."

Dr. John just looked at me.

"Gemma isn't as skinny as I am, but she's beautiful. So are some of the other girls I saw today." I said, once again sounding confused. It was like I was trying to figure out a puzzle.

Dr. John gave me an encouraging smile. "Yes, very good Emily."

Tears filled my eyes as the realization slowly dawned on me. "I am sick. Aren't I? I'm fucked up, I'm not normal." I said through choked sobs. Crying seemed to be my thing these days.

"You are sick, yes. That's why you're here." Dr. John said softly. "What made you realize this Emily?"

I sniffled. "I never took notice to other people before, because of Darren I was so focused on myself and how I looked. Today I got to look at other people. Other girls. I see them as beautiful, but they aren't skinny like me. When I look in the mirror, I don't see what everyone else sees. I see a body covered in fat. I can't help it."

Dr. John nodded. "Very good, Emily. Very good. I wasn't expecting you to realize this so soon. I was expecting you to be how you were in the hospital."

I laughed, remembering how stubborn I could be. "I guess actually noticing other people's appearances made me realize it. But Dr. John, I don't want to be sick…" I said helplessly. "I want to go home. To Darren."

Dr. John shook his head, and started rubbing his temples. "Emily, even when you do go home, you will not be seeing Darren." He said matter-of-factly.

"Why not?!" I asked angrily.

"He's the reason you're here in the first place. Seeing him when you get home will put you right back in here." He said sternly.

I crossed my arms over my chest, and refused to look at him.

"Why don't we talk about some of the kids you've met so far today?" he asked politely, as though he didn't just crush my hopes and dreams.

I didn't answer right away, then finally I gave in and said "I only actually met three people, besides Gemma. Leila, Anna and Caleb." I rolled my eyes as I said Caleb's name.

"I see. Do you like any of them?"

"I guess. Leila seemed nice, Anna was shy and Caleb…he's intimidating." I concluded.

Dr. John laughed. "Why do you say that?"

"I don't know!" I said slightly offended by his laughter. "He's so tall, and he has a tattoo and he's awfully confident for someone in a mental hospital."

"Maybe Caleb is further down the road to recovery than you?" Dr. John pointed out.

"Maybe." I said simply. My thoughts were wandering off to Darren. His blue eyes sparkling all the time. I smiled.

"Emily?"

I shook my head, "Sorry, just thinking."

"About?"

"Nothing." I said quickly, avoiding looking Dr. John in the eyes.

He nodded but didn't press me further. We sat in silence for a couple of minutes.

"Dr. John, what am I allowed to do after this?" I asked. I wasn't sure what all of the rules were yet.

"Well," he said "You can go back to your home, and hang out until dinner, or you can go to the rec room or you can sit out in the courtyard."

I nodded, considering my options. I really wanted to ask Gemma why she was here. Maybe we could go sit in the court yard and talk. Yes, that's what I would do. My time was up, and we agreed I would be back on Wednesday. I actually liked that I was still seeing Dr. John because I was comfortable with him, and if I had someone new I was sure I would sit there not saying anything for a whole hour.

Caleb was standing outside of the door and we started walking back to my room in silence. After about a minute or so, I randomly said, "I realized I'm sick" in a small voice that didn't sound like me. I had no clue why I was telling him this. I barely knew him at all.

"Oh yeah? Good for you. That saves you a lot of silent sessions." He patted me awkwardly on the shoulder.

"Why are you here?" I asked, hoping I would get lucky and he would tell me. I knew it was a long shot though.

"Sorry darling, I don't think that's any of your business just yet. Anyway, here we are. Your room. Unless there's another place you'd like to go?"

peered in. Gemma wasn't here. Huh. "Do you know where Gemma is?" I asked him.

"Yeah, she's in her therapy session. Just went there actually. Listen, instead of sitting in our room all alone, why not join me in the rec room for a game of pool?" he asked hopefully.

shook my head. "No thanks. I have lots to think about. Plus I want to be here when Gemma gets back. But thank you…seriously." I put my hand on his arm, but pulled back right away.

"No problem. We're usually always down there though, you're welcome to join us anytime." He waved and walked down the hall to the rec room where I could guys whooping at his presence.

I flopped down on my bed and grabbed my teddy bear; the one my mom got me at the hospital. I hugged him tight and rested my head on my pillow. Thoughts of Darren were still reeling in my head, and for once I wish I wouldn't think about him. I had other things to focus on; like how I was going to start my conversation with Gemma about why she was here. This only led to her words and Caleb words haunting me. *You're fucked up, just like the rest of us. They don't send sane people here.* I put my hands over my ears as if this were going to make the voices in my head stop. I started to cry, remembering when I finally said out loud that I am sick. I am here because I am not normal. I can't go to a friend's house whenever I please. I can't go to dance class like I did just weeks ago. I couldn't go with my mom to visit my Grandma on a Sunday morning. My life had not been normal for a while and I didn't even realize it.

I hadn't been out with friends in months. I don't even know when I lost my social life to be honest. I became obsessed with working out and anticipating dance class just to see Darren. Leah was always asking me to go to the movies and sleep over and grab a bite to eat and I always found an excuse to say no.

I began crying harder as I realized how simple and boring my life had become. I let being skinny control my entire life, and I was completely out of control now. I had to be fed through a fucking tube because I didn't want to eat on my own. I almost died twice in a matter of weeks. I really needed to get my act together. How I would start to do that, I had no idea. Food still sent me into a panic attack. I was sure I wouldn't be able to exercise here. I didn't know how I was going to handle this, but I had to figure out something.

I managed to stop crying and it was a good thing I did because Gemma came back a couple minutes later.

"Are you okay?" she asked tentatively. I hadn't moved out of the fetal position on my bed, and I was still hugging my teddy bear. I'm pretty sure my face was red and blotchy, and my eyes still shining with tears. I rolled over to face her. She was standing in the door way, shifting her body weight uncomfortably.

I sat up. "Yeah. I'm fine. I think." I said groggily.

"I was going to go to the rec room but I could hear you crying from down the hall. Which by the way, just remember to close the door? It's more beneficial for you if you do. Do you want to talk about it?" she asked as she sat down on the end of my bed. Her eyes were wide, and had fear in them.

I shook my head. "I uhm, I realized you were right…I am messed up like the rest of you. I belong here…" I said, hanging my head.

Gemma drew in a sharp breath, and put her hand on my knee. Her hands were ice cold. "How did you realize this?"

I looked up at her and stared for a moment. "I noticed how beautiful you are and some of the other girls too. You're not skinny like me though, but you're still beautiful." I said quietly, my voice full of shame. It was bad enough I talked about it with Dr. John.

Gemma smiled a small smile and said "Thank you, Emily. For thinking I'm beautiful. I'm glad you realized that you need to be here." Her voice was soft and kind, but shaky as well. Her eyes were glistening with tears and I could tell she was truly thankful for my comment.

I had completely forgotten my desire to know why she was here. It didn't matter much, I realized. Everyone had a reason to be here and that was enough for me. Gemma didn't seem to think so though because she started to roll up the sleeves of her shirt, and I gasped, finally seeing why she was here.

Scars. White, pink, red, scabbed, lines all over her arms. Some were small, some were long and some looked as though they had been deep. Gemma lifted her shirt up to the bottom of bosom, and more scars covered her stomach and hips. This poor girl. I didn't want to imagine what had made her do this to herself.

"This is why I'm here Emily." She said quietly, not bothering to cover her scars back up. "It took me half a year to admit that I needed to be here. I found ways to cut at least once a week. I can't tell you how many times I got sent to the isolation room. I was bad. For the past six months I've been getting better and I've really proved myself to everyone here."

A tear shed down my cheek, and I reached out and took her hand in mine. "I don't know what made you do this Gemma, but I still think you're beautiful." I said softly.

Gemma blinked back tears and let go of my hand. She stood up and shut the door then sat back down on my bed and folded her knees to her chest. "My pop used to beat me." She whispered.

I looked over at her, and her face was covered in pain and anger. I didn't know what to say, and luckily Gemma continued. "Nothing I ever did was good enough, ya know? There was always something wrong, and it was always my fault. He really made me feel like a piece of shit. He had been screaming at me, and spanking me, like he usually did, and I couldn't take it anymore. When he left my room, I grabbed a pair of scissors and just sliced the blade across my wrist. It just went downhill from there."

I wrapped my arm around her, as if to protect her from the terrible memory. Her voice was shaking the whole time she spoke and I could tell she was trying not to hold back tears. "That's over now, Gemma." I said reassuringly.

"I know. I don't want to talk about it anymore though, okay? I don't like thinking about it." She said flatly, though she still stayed sitting next to me.

"Okay." I said.

We sat like that for a while. She didn't ask me anymore about what was wrong, or why I don't eat. I didn't ask her anymore about her cuts. We simply just sat on my bed in silence, lost in our own thoughts. Was this what it was like to have a friend? I couldn't remember.

Gemma looked at her watch and jumped off the bed. "Shit! Dinner starts soon! Come on!" she yelped.

I sat on my bed, just staring at her, scared out of my mind. "I can't." I whimpered.

"You have no choice actually. ED girls have to go to all meals. Now c'mon!" she said in a motherly fashion and pulled me off my bed. I noticed how her shirt hugged her arms, so there was no chance her sleeves would slip up. I still couldn't understand why anyone would want to hurt Gemma. She was like a porcelain doll. Her pale, ivory skin, long, black hair and pale green eyes. She was precious.

Reluctantly, I walked with her to the cafeteria and we took seats next to Leila and Anna. There were three other girls sitting across from us but I didn't know who they were. I didn't have a chance to learn their names before our table was dismissed to get our dinner. We were having pork chops with mashed potatoes and gravy with corn bread. My heart started racing, and I could feel my face getting hot. I saw Dr. John standing at the end of the line, talking to some lady. I grabbed a tray and rushed to him.

"Dr. John," I said desperately. "Do I have to eat all of this?"

"No, Emily, you do not. You may not skip meals, but you are not required to eat a whole meal, yet. Your stomach is still too small." He said calmly.

My heart beat slowed, and I was calm again. I nodded and returned to my seat next to Gemma. I looked down at my tray. I didn't know what to try and eat first. I learned that the other three girls' names were Liz, Hannah, and Mia. I didn't pay much attention to the conversation though. I was too preoccupied by the food mocking me on the tray.

I picked off a corner of the corn bread and nibbled on it. It was sweet, and soft. I swallowed. I debated on taking another bite, and decided to take another nibble. By the time dinner hour was up, I had eaten an entire corner of the corn bread and a very small bite of mashed potatoes. My pork chops stayed untouched, and my glass of water was almost completely gone. Dr. John came by my table and gave me a meek smile before wandering off again. I wondered if he was proud of me; I would have to wait until Wednesday to find out though.

Gemma asked if I wanted to go back to the rec room with everyone and I agreed. It was better than sitting in my room by myself. We went to the couch and started watching The Big Bang Theory. I used to be obsessed with this show, before I became obsessed with

losing weight. Caleb sat down next to me on the couch and said "Hey" before focusing on the T.V. I looked over at him, wondering why he decided to sit next to me of all places, he was normally playing pool. He felt me looking at him, because he turned his head towards me and said "What?" looking completely puzzled.

"I was just wondering why you're sitting here, and not playing pool." I said coolly. To be truthful, his comment about sane people stung me earlier, even if it was true. Not that Gemma's didn't, because it did, it's just, I don't know, I found it easier to be mean to Caleb.

He shrugged. "I like this show. Plus I do do other things than play pool, you know." He said with a smirk. "Why? Does it bother you that I'm sitting here?" he asked, pretending to sound wounded, and putting his hand on his heart.

I let out a reluctant giggle and said "No, I was just curious."

"Curiosity killed the cat." He said simply, turning his attention back to the T.V. screen.

I stared at his silhouette and smiled to myself, then turned my gaze back to the T.V. I could feel Gemma looking at me but I didn't pay attention to her. The three of us sat in silence, watching Big Bang Theory until it was 9:30 and everybody needed to start heading back to their rooms for lights out. Caleb said good-bye to us both and walked the opposite way down the hall to his room. I liked the way his hips swung when he walked. Then I thought, *it's a good thing Darren couldn't hear my thoughts.* I am so messed up.

Chapter 4

Gemma smiled at me the following morning, no matter how many times I told her to stop.

"Caleb likes youuuuuu." She teased as we were getting dressed. We were quite a sight to see, us two, naked. Gem was covered in scars and I had no meat to my body.

I blushed, but thankfully she couldn't see. "He does not." I said nonchalantly. "He's my escort, it's perfectly natural for us to talk."

She gave me a you're-full-of-shit look and said "That's not what you thought last night when he sat down next to you."

I rolled my eyes. "I just wasn't expecting him to talk to me other than when he was walking me somewhere, but there's nothing wrong with it."

"Mhmm." I could tell she didn't believe me.

We were both dressed and walked down to the cafeteria today. I barely touched my French toast, eggs and bacon. It wasn't so much that I was scared to eat it, I was nervous

because I had my first group session today and I wasn't sure what to expect. I only took a bite or two of my bacon, and a mouthful of scrambled eggs. I nibbled a tiny corner off the French toast, and that was it. I felt sick to my stomach, I was so anxious.

Gemma assured me that I would be fine, and not to think about it too much. Leila told me that Group had become the favorite part of her day, and Anna didn't say much because she was well…Anna. I made a mental note to try and talk to her, because it seemed like everyone else just ignored her and didn't bother with her. Caleb came over to my table and asked where I wanted to go. Group wasn't until five o'clock tonight, and my stomach churned at the thought that I still had to get through lunch and the afternoon. I asked Caleb if we could go to the courtyard, I needed some fresh air. I asked Gemma if she was coming with me, but she said she had a headache and was going to take a nap. I knew she was lying, she just wanted me to have alone time with Caleb, but I couldn't say anything.

Caleb and I walked silently to the courtyard and he asked if I wanted him to stay with me.

"Only if you want to." I said, looking up at him. He was blocking the sun perfectly, and I was hoping he didn't move. I didn't notice before but his black hair had a bit of a copper tint to it. It was somewhat humid outside today, but then again, it was the middle of August. The courtyard really was cute. It had a little garden filled with flowers of all kinds and colors. There were some picnic tables and benches you could sit down at, and a small fountain in the middle of it all. Thankfully there were trees that provided some shade, to get you out of the sun's warmth. Caleb and I chose a picnic table directly underneath a tree.

"Are you sure you don't mind staying?" I asked nervously, as he glanced around. All I could smell was honeysuckle and the grass.

"I don't one bit. I don't have anywhere to go until about noon." He said, looking me right in the eyes. His eyes were beautiful. I noticed they weren't black, but a warm, smooth, chocolate brown. He smiled briefly then looked away from me again.

"Why did you get your tattoo?" I asked. I noticed it said the word "Strength."

He looked back at me, squinting slightly because of the sun. "I'd have to tell you why I'm here, and I don't think I want to do that just yet." He said with a tone that I knew meant he was serious. I shut my mouth, and I took the opportunity to look around the courtyard some more.

"I'm sorry I questioned you last night. You know, when you came to watch T.V." I said, my voice filled with embarrassment.

Caleb chuckled. "It's okay. I understand. You don't really know me. I guess I would have reacted the same way."

I smiled. At least he didn't think I was a bitch or a psycho. Even though we sat in silence, it was a comfortable silence, like with Gem. We made a comment every once in a while about a butterfly that passed by, or a bird that would perch itself on the edge of the fountain for a drink. It was starting to get warmer though, as the morning neared closer to noon. Beads of sweat were starting to form on Caleb's forehead and above his lip. I smiled to myself as I watched him wipe them away.

"I told Gemma last night, I realized that I am sick and that I do belong here." I said, my voice quavering.

Caleb turned his gaze back to me, and looked as though he never saw me before. His expression softened, and his mouth spread into a smile. His teeth really were perfect.

"What took you so long?" he half laughed.

I reached across the table and playfully shoved his arm. "Shut up. Gemma told me it took her six months to realize she needed to be here."

"There's a difference between you and Gemma."

I looked at him, puzzled.

"You already knew you needed to be here, you just didn't want to accept it." He said matter-of-factly. He stood up, and extended his hand out to me. I took it and stood as well. This was our cue that it was time to go back inside, and Caleb had to go. I frowned as he walked slightly in front of me, considering what he had just said.

asked Caleb to take me to the rec room so I could at least be distracted until lunch. Once here, the guys taught me how to play pool. I learned some of their names too. Jason had been here the longest of the guys, coming up on a year and a half, and Alex was the newest, having only been here two and a half weeks. Alex was shy like Anna. I liked everyone I met so far.

Lunch wasn't as bad as I thought it would be. Today we had spaghetti and meatballs with a little side salad and garlic bread. I managed to eat half of my salad, two bites of my bread, and one forkful of spaghetti. Gemma nodded encouragingly as I hesitated to take the forkful, reassuring me I wouldn't blow up like a whale.

Five o'clock finally rolled around, and I found myself sitting in a big room, with bean bag chairs forming a giant circle in the middle of the room. There was a lady sitting in one of them, looking down at a clip board, muttering to herself. She had dirty blonde hair that was half pulled up, and she was in a chocolate blazer and a pair of jeans. I assumed she was the group leader. I was the only one in the room so far so I nervously walked up to her and cleared my throat.

"Oh!" she said. "Hello dear, I'm Lisa; I'm your Group leader. You can take a seat anywhere you like, as soon as you tell me your name." she smiled up at me. Her hazel eyes sparkled, and so did her lip gloss.

I found it hard to find my words and it took me a second to remember my name. "Emily." I said quietly.

Lisa looked down at her list and her eyes searched the paper until she found my name and crossed it off with her pen. "Alright! You can pick any chair you want, Emily!" she said brightly.

I turned and picked one almost directly opposite from Lisa, but one that wouldn't leave me looking straight at her. I glanced around nervously, noticing there really wasn't decoration to the room. No tacky posters or paintings. Just bland, white walls. The outside view wasn't much better either; all you could see were factories across the street, and the staff parking lot.

Kids started coming in and checking in with Lisa, filling in the empty chairs around me. Hey wait! Gemma just walked in! She told me she didn't have group the same time as me! I frowned, stood up and met her in the middle of the circle.

"I thought we weren't in the same group?" I asked, slightly annoyed.

She rolled her eyes. "Em, if I had told you we were, you wouldn't have taken the time to realize you need to be here, because you could have waited until today to figure out why I'm here." She said it as if I should have known this the whole time.

I stuck my tongue out at her and we walked back to where I had been sitting, and she took her place next to me.

"You have to tell me about your time with Caleb today, by the way." She whispered, and winked at me.

I shoved her away. "There's nothing to tell." I whispered back.

I only recognized Anna and Alex, everyone else I didn't know. Lisa stood up and cleared her throat, telling everyone we needed to be quiet.

"Okay everyone, we have a new member joining us today, so we are going to say our names and why we are here. We must also remember the rules. No talking while someone is talking. Be respectful of everyone's opinions, and stories. Positive comments only." She raised an eyebrow on the last rule, and I gulped, praying the group didn't have an issue with negative comments. Lisa sat back down in her bean bag chair and told the girl on her left to go first.

"Well, I'm Rebecca and I'm here because I got into too many fights in school." I tried to hide the shock on my face. I could definitely see the bully in her. I made a mental note not to mess with her.

Alex was next, and his voice was barely audible over the silent room. "I'm Alex, and I'm here because my brother verbally and mentally abused me." My heart ached for him. He was so small and fragile.

Courtney was here because her grandma caught her stealing her prescription pills to get high. Allison was here because she suffered from bi-polar disorder. Eric was here because he had anger management issues gone wild. Tyler was here because he was raped by his mom's friend. Anna stayed silent.

Then it was my turn. I looked around at everyone. I didn't know how to word mine. Did I mention Darren? No! Don't do that! I cleared my throat. "I'm Emily, and I starve myself to be beautiful." I looked around for reactions, some people looked sad for me, and at least two other people looked like they knew exactly what I was taking about.

Gemma announced why she was here. Then it was a kid named Chase's turn, he was here for doing hardcore drugs. A girl named Jesse turned out to starve herself too, although she used the word "Anorexic". Beth was here for burning herself, and Mike was here for beating up his step-dad. The last girl of the group, Harmony starved herself as well.

Today's discussion was why we got into the habits we have now. Oh God, okay, I could always make up something. I couldn't talk about Darren, at least not the full story.

Most of the stories involved being bullied, or their parents ignored them, or their parents got divorced or someone died. It was my turn before I knew it.

"Uhm. My dad left my mom and I when I was two." Is what I ended up saying. I was bewildered with myself. No one would see any reason why that would cause someone to become anorexic. "My mom still won't tell me why he left. I've been wondering since I was five." My voice was starting to shake and I hoped that my answer had sufficed. Gemma had grabbed hold of my hand and gave me a reassuring look.

She then went on to talk about being abused by her dad. Her voice didn't shake as much as when she told me, and I was proud of her.

The rest of the session was filled by people talking about their first few weeks here, to help make me feel better I suppose. I learned that Chase broke a few windows out of anger. Jesse cried herself to sleep for almost a month and it took her at least two or three weeks for her to talk in Group. Alex was still pretty new so it was comforting for him too.

I was feeling okay by the end of Group and I had decided it wouldn't be that bad. I told Gemma to go ahead, and to tell Caleb I would be out in a minute. I caught up with Anna

as she approached the door way. "Hey, Anna, I just wanted to say if you ever want to talk, I'm a really good listener. You can ask Gemma." I said with a smile.

She returned the smile but it faded quickly. "Thanks, Emily, really, but I'm not much of a talker." Her voice was sad, and quiet. She continued to walk out of the room to meet up with her escort. I stared after her, determined to get her to talk one day. Caleb was waiting outside for me and welcomed me with a smile.

"How was your first Group?" he asked.

"It was better than I expected." I let out a big sigh. "Everyone was really friendly and welcoming and it was…not scary." I concluded.

Caleb laughed. I liked his laugh. "You're cute, Emily." I blushed, and thankfully he didn't actually look at me, so he didn't notice. I couldn't help but smile.

I didn't eat much of my dinner. I felt full from lunch still. Thankfully it was chicken noodle soup with crackers and another small salad. I managed a couple spoonfuls of soup before deciding I was done. Gemma looked over at me and frowned. "You're not even touching your salad? Or a cracker?" she asked, her spoon midway to her mouth.

I shook my head. "I feel full from lunch." I said. Leila eyed me, but quickly glanced back down at her own tray. Leila had been here for a little over a year now, and was okay with eating more than I was. She had finished her salad and half of her soup. Her crackers would remain untouched. She didn't have any right to yell at me though. I told Gemma I didn't feel well and told her I was going to find Caleb and ask him to take me back to our room. She looked at me suspiciously but nodded in approval anymore. I took my tray up to the counter and turned to find Caleb's table. Once I found it, I walked over and asked him if he could take me back to my room. He looked at me, worried. "Are you okay?" he asked with a frown.

"I just don't feel well that's all." I said lightly.

"Do you want to go to the nurse?" he asked, lightly touching my elbow, completely facing me now.

I shook my head. "No, I think I just need to go lay down or something."

"Okay."

We started walking out of the cafeteria and before I knew it I was scooped up in Caleb's arms.

"What. Are. You. Doing?!" I shrieked, struggling against his grip, but it was no use. He was much stronger than me.

"You said you don't feel well, so I'm carrying you back to your room. I don't need you collapsing in the hallway or anything." He said darkly. I smiled because he really did care.

We got to my room, and I looked at him with my eyes wide and pleading. "Can you…uhm…escort me to the bathroom? I think if I take a shower it'll help me feel better." I added a smile.

He rolled his eyes, and I knew his answer was yes. I grabbed my things and this time we walked arm in arm down the showers. There was a supervisor stationed just inside the door. She stopped me when I walked in. "Are you an ED girl?" she asked, her tone serious.

I nodded. "Okay." She said. I turned on one of the showers, undressed and stepped in. The sound of my shower wasn't that loud, but soon someone else came in to shower and together they created enough noise to cover up anything else. I took my chance, bending as low as I could to the drain, and stuck my finger to my throat. My gag reflexes sucked, coming in handy for this type of thing. My breakfast, lunch and dinner came right back up and I felt light again. I stood up and smiled. I barely made any noise anyway, and with the water there's no way she heard me. I finished my shower quickly, remembering Caleb had to escort me back.

Ten minutes later I was showered and dressed and back with Caleb. I felt okay for the first time since I got here. I was in the middle of talking when Caleb stopped me mid-sentence and leaned in close to my face.

"What are you doing?" I asked, slightly annoyed.

He drew back, and glared at me. "You threw up in the shower." He said accusingly.

A look of shock and fear flickered over my face but I quickly replaced it with anger. "No!" I said defiantly.

"Yes you did. I can smell it on your breath." His voice was starting to rise.

"Shhh!" I whisper yelled. "Do you want our conversation to be heard?" I asked angrily. My face was getting hot, and Caleb was still glaring at me. His brows furrowed together, and his mouth in a slight frown. His eyes squinting at me, taking me in.

"Technically, I should report you." His voice was icy, and threatening. I felt my blood run cold.

"No," I pleaded, stepping towards him. "Please don't."

He stepped back, but continued to stare at me. I looked back at him, my eyes wide with fear and my body shaking. The hallway was deserted except for me and him. Everyone was in the rec room or their bedrooms. Finally, he sighed.

"I won't report you this time. But next time, I'm not hesitating." He pointed a finger warningly at me. "Now come on. Let's get you to bed."

I didn't argue as he picked me up and carried me to my room.

Gemma was curled up on her bed, with a lamp on, reading a book. She seemed in her own little world, so I didn't bother saying anything. I shut our door, and climbed into my own bed. I lay looking up at my ceiling, thinking about everything from today.

Caleb really was a nice guy, and I knew he was just looking out for me. Besides, it was my fault for throwing up my meals in the first place. I made a promise to myself that there wouldn't have to be a next time for Caleb to report me. I just hope I could stick to it.

My thoughts changed to Anna and Alex. Alex had to be at least fourteen, poor guy. He's always so timid and shy; I hope he opens up while he's here. I wanted to figure out what happened with Anna though. The only person she talks to, that I've seen is Leila; she doesn't even talk to Gemma that much.

Gemma. I didn't expect to make any friends when I first arrived yesterday, but I could proudly say Gemma was becoming my friend. I constantly thought about why anyone would want to hurt her, especially so badly that she wanted to hurt herself. The thought made me want to cry, and I tried to push the thoughts out of my head.

I thought back to my normal life schedule, before I was trapped here. Today was Tuesday which meant I would have been at dance class; with Darren watching my every move. It was almost nine o'clock now, and dance class was just ending, which means I would have been getting my "special treatment" from Darren soon. I shuddered at the thought. I could feel his eyes on me even though he was miles and miles away; it gave me goose bumps. This wasn't a safe topic either.

"Hey Emily?" Gemma's voice called from the other side of the room. She had put down her magazine and was sitting upright now. Her voice sounded tight, and I could tell she was fighting back tears.

"Yeah?" I responded.

"Can I…can I tell you stories about my dad?" she asked hesitantly. I could hear the uncertainty in her voice, second guessing if she actually wanted to do this. She was biting her bottom lip, and her green eyes were swelling with unshed tears.

I sat up also, and went to sit next to her. I could feel her shaking slightly. "Only if you want to." I whispered softly.

We sat back against the wall, pillows in our laps and she began to talk. I didn't question why she suddenly wanted to talk about it, because it didn't matter. Gemma needed someone to listen, and I was happy to be here for her.

"I don't really understand how it started. I just remember I came home from a friend's house in 9th grade, and I had forgotten to do my list of chores, and my dad was really angry. He had guests coming over that day, and since my chores weren't done, the house was somewhat of a mess. I just managed to walk in the door before he started yelling at me; telling me I was going to embarrass him in front of his guests, make him to be some sort of slob, and all of this other bullshit. I tried telling him to relax, that I would get the chores done quickly and then he'd have nothing to worry about, but he didn't want to hear about it. He was so angry, and at first I don't think he meant to do it, because he looked shocked afterwards, but that faded quickly. He slapped me so hard that I nearly fell to the floor, and my cheek was stinging, and tears were rolling down my cheek. I looked up at my dad and for about two seconds, I saw shock on his face, but it was replaced by satisfaction. He picked me up by the collar of my shirt, and told me to stay upstairs for the rest of the day. I ran as quickly as I could and cried for hours." She finished with a heavy sigh, and her cheeks were stained with tears and mascara. Her lips were trembling still, and I had been holding her hand through most of her story.

"Gemma…you know you didn't deserve that. You didn't deserve any of the beatings you've gotten." I said, squeezing her hand. I must make her know this. She feels so worthless and she's not. She's not at all. "You helped me realize why I'm here." I whispered. She finally looked at me, her eyes still watering and she smiled.

"It's weird. I feel worthless and not worthless at the same time, you know? I don't quite know how to explain it." She laughed when she said this, and wiped a tear that was making its way down her pale cheek.

I smiled back. "I know what you mean." Truly, I did. I knew there were things I didn't deserve to go through, and at other times I felt like I deserved every horrible thing that's happened to me.

I don't what brought it on but we both just started laughing. We laughed until our faces were purple, our eyes were filled with tears and our sides were crippling with pain. After we finally stopped laughing, Gemma resumed a somewhat serious face.

"You know," she said, looking at me with a sad expression. "Caleb likes you."

I shook my head, and tried brushing it off, but deep down I knew she was right. I wasn't ready to admit that though. "I don't think so. He's my escort, and he's just been doing his job."

"No, Emily, he does. He likes you a lot. I can see it when he looks at you. It's quite beautiful, actually." She smiled to herself.

I looked at her, confused. I didn't understand why we were talking about all of this.

"Gemma, look, even if Caleb does like me, I don't like him, at least not like that. He's a really nice guy, and he's helpful, but I just don't like him that way." I said firmly. I didn't want to talk about this anymore.

This time it was Gemma who shook her head. "Emily, long before I came here, I had a boyfriend. We dated for eight months, and he told me he loved me. I decided I could trust him enough to show him my cuts. So I did…" she paused, drawing in a breath. "and he told me I was a freak and left. I never heard from him again." She said sadly. "I really loved him, Emily." She wasn't crying this time, but I could tell she was still hurting from it.

"Caleb likes you, a lot. He likes you despite of you being sick, of your imperfections, don't let that slip away, because there's not many guys like that out there."

"Gemma, I already have someone back home…" I said, not looking her in the eye.

"Does he love you?"

I paused for a moment. "He says he does…" I said softly.

"Does he love you for all of you? Because if he doesn't…it's time you cut him loose. I'm also warning you. Caleb and I are good friends. He's been through a lot, just like the rest of us. So don't lead him on if you don't like him, okay? Don't mess with his feelings." I could hear how much she cared for him in the way she spoke.

She started adjusting herself so that she was laying down, telling me it was time to move to my bed again. I turned off the light before making my way to my bed, and found my way through the darkness. I climbed into my own bed, snuggling down into the sheets, feeling a slight warmth wash over me. I felt comfortable, and at ease for the first time in a very long time. I heard Gemma adjust herself, and looked over at her silhouette. I thought about what she had said; about Darren, and loving all of me, and made a mental note to talk about it with Dr. John tomorrow.

To my surprise, I wasn't seeing sparkling blue eyes before I drifted off to sleep, instead I was seeing warm, brown eyes. I shook the image out of my head and rolled over, hoping to fall asleep.

The next morning, I woke earlier than usual, but had no choice but to lay in bed until it was time to go to breakfast. Gemma was sleeping soundly five feet away from me, and I envied her in that moment. My dreams were unsettling, and I kept waking up throughout the night.

I managed to drift off to sleep again for a little while, and woke back up at 8:30, which was enough time to get out of bed, dress and wait for Caleb to come get me and go to breakfast.

Nine o'clock was here before I knew it, and Caleb was standing in my door way. Gemma had already gone down to breakfast a couple minutes ago. He looked exhausted, and I went to ask him why but the first thing he said was, "I'm not in the mood for any talking." I raised my eyebrows at him, even though he wasn't looking at me.

Our short walk to the cafeteria was silent, since I couldn't talk, and he went right to his table as soon as we got inside the cafeteria. I went to the line to get my pancakes and bacon. I was actually hungry and wanted to test how much I could eat before I felt guilty.

I got back to the table and was relieved to find that all of the girls were in a good mood. Leila was chatting about her visit with her mom last night, and Anna was listening intently, while mindlessly chewing on a piece of bacon. Liz asked me how I liked Group yesterday and I admitted that it really wasn't that bad. Mia and Hannah were talking about an intense game of monopoly they had gotten into the night before. Gemma interjected into mine and Liz's conversation between bites of her breakfast. Towards the end of lunch, my table congratulated me for eating one whole pancake. They weren't big pancakes, but it was the best I had done all week. I felt proud of myself too.

Later that day, I was back in Dr. John's office, and for the first time, I was so happy to be here.

"I have to say Emily, I'm really proud of you after breakfast this morning. You are doing fantastic!" his mouth split into a grin as he spoke, and excitement filled his voice. I couldn't help but smile too.

"Thank you, I was proud of me too. Dr. John is it okay if we talk about something of my choice today? I need to get it off my chest." I said with a sigh. My conversation with Gemma the night before had been haunting me ever since.

"Certainly, that's why you come here." He said calmly, folding his hands in his lap, and leaning back in his chair.

"Gemma and I were talking last night, and we started talking about Caleb…" I couldn't say his name without blushing and it bothered me.

Dr. John smiled and said "Go on."

"Well, Gemma told me that Caleb likes me, and I know that, but I don't like him back. I told Gemma that, and I told Gemma I already love someone, and she made a point that I hadn't thought about, and it's been bothering me ever since."

"What was it that she said?"

"She said that Caleb likes me for all of me, my imperfections, my sickness. He likes all of that, and that I won't find a lot of boys like that. Then she asked if the boy back home loves me for all of me, and it got me thinking…"

"Got you thinking what, Emily?"

A tear shed down my cheek, but I didn't bother wiping it away. "Darren doesn't love me for all of me. If he did…he wouldn't have made me do this to myself." I finally said. More tears were falling now but I didn't care. "Can I- can I talk more about what happened between me and Darren?"

"If you want to, Emily. Of course, we'll discuss everything afterwards." He said nicely.

I nodded, and took a deep breath.

Darren had been giving me his "special treatment" for almost two months now, and I wasn't too fond of it anymore. I found that he was rather forceful, and quite more powerful than I. It was unnerving. So far his special treatment was just giving me a kiss before I left his office after checking my weight, but he always held me so tightly. I didn't know what to say either.

Darren was becoming more and more pleased with me each week because I kept losing weight. I was finally down to 110 like he wanted me to be, and he said he had a special something planned. I was more nervous than excited by this point.

As usual, I showered quickly and changed into my normal clothes. It was unusually warm for a mid-October day, and I had worn a skirt and sweater here, and it felt good to have it back on. I knocked on Darren's office door and waited for him to open the door. My nerves were exploding inside of me, and I just wanted to get this over with.

As soon as Darren opened the door, I knew this time would be completely different from all of the others. His eyes had this unfamiliar, dangerous sparkle to them. I slowly walked in and took my usual spot in the chair in front of his desk. He stood in front of me, and looked down on me. It made me nervous. He was so much taller than I was, and his muscles seemed to be bulging out of his shirt today.

"Congratulations, sweetheart. You finally did it." He said softly. His voice was so low, I could barely hear him. "Come closer."

I was unsure whether it was best to obey, or try and get out at this point, so I went with obey until I thought of a way to get out. I moved inches closer, so I could feel Darren's hot breath on my face, and his eyes were fixated on mine.

Like usual, he leaned in to kiss me. His hand found the back of my neck, and his other hand went to the small of my back. I moaned in the back of my throat, because this kiss was different. It was deep, and hard and persistent. I didn't like it, but I couldn't get out

of his grip. He pushed his tongue into my mouth, and explored. As good as his skills were, I wanted him to stop. I tried to push him away but I couldn't manage. Not eating was making me weak; I was defenseless, and I was sure that Darren knew this.

His mouth moved to my cheek and down to my neck. This was already going farther than it ever had before. He trailed his mouth down my neck, his breath hot and his lips moist. I tried to ignore the fact that it felt good, and concentrated on not wanting him to do this. I realized my mouth was now free and took my opportunity.

"Darren," my voice was squeaky, and timid. "Please stop..."

"You know you like it, baby. Just relax. I'll help you." He said into my hair, which his hand was now fisted in. He pushed me up against his desk, and his hand that had been on my back was now traveling to my chest, beginning to fondle my breasts. I moaned again, half in pleasure and half in helplessness.

"Please, just stop." I pleaded.

Darren gripped my hair harder, and began to pull off my sweater with his free hand. I don't know how he did it. He freed my breasts from my bra, and began to suck on my nipples, his other hand now traveling up and down my bare legs. I wanted this and I didn't want this, but I didn't know which I wanted more. If this was going to stop, I had to stop it soon.

"Darren," I tried to say more firmly. "Stop it. I don't want this." My voice still sounded weak, and Darren was to blame. His mouth just felt so good against my skin.

He stopped what he was doing though, as I spoke. "Do you love me?" he asked harshly, still gripping my hair.

I whimpered. "Yes."

"Then you'll do this with me. I love you, and you love me. This is what people do when they love each other." He said, looking me in the eyes. I had lost this battle. I still didn't want this, but I wasn't going to win.

Darren had pushed everything off of his desk, and forced me on top of it, with him on top of me. He was back to kissing me again, his hands working my skirt off of me. When my skirt was off, he took one of his hands to hold down both of mine and fished around for something in his drawer. He pulled out a role of duct tape. He taped down my hands one by one, and looked satisfied and hungry when he was done.

"You're finally beautiful. I've been waiting for this for so long, Emily." He said softly. His hands were traveling down my body, and his mouth was back at my neck again. He trailed soft, small kisses all the way from my neck, to each of my breasts again. His body was pressed against mine; there was no way I could move. He moved from my breasts to

I fixed my hair, and walked out of the office, finally releasing my tears.

I looked back up at Dr. John, who was staring at me with his mouth slightly open.

"Emily. He.."

"Darren raped me." I said through a choked sob, finishing his sentence for him.

Chapter 5

I wasn't ready to tell Gemma about Darren yet, even though she had told me about her father last night. I just admitted to Dr. John that Darren raped me; there was no way I was re-telling my story right now. I knew Gemma would ask though. She would ask how my session went with Dr. John but I just didn't want to talk about it. I hoped she would understand.

Caleb was waiting for outside of the door and I gave him a small smile before we started walking. He seemed to be in a better mood because he returned my smile and asked, "How are you?"

I didn't know how to answer that question, so I settled on, "I'm not really sure."

"Do you want to talk about it?" he sounded concerned, as he looped his arm through mine. It felt natural. Our pace was slow, as we were no hurry to get anywhere.

I shook my head vigorously. "No, I don't." I said firmly.

"Okay." He said. "Do you want to play a game of pool? It usually takes my mind off of things."

"I don't know how to play though."

"It's okay, I'll teach you." He smiled at me. There was no way I could say no.

"Okay." I said, slightly flustered. I could feel a blush creeping up my neck.

We reached the rec room, and I didn't bother looking for Gemma because I knew she wouldn't be there. Instead, Caleb directed me to the pool table, and handed me a pole cue, and started explaining the rules to me.

Thirty minutes later, I was beating him. He kept asking me if I was hustling him, but I didn't even know what that meant. It really was a good time. My session with Dr. John was slowly fading away, and Caleb was making me laugh with his endless supply of corny jokes. It had finally come down the eight ball. I had been solids, and he was stripes. I lined up my shot, called it on the top right corner pocket, and sunk it first try! I won!

Caleb hung his head in defeat, but only briefly, before pulling me in for a congratulatory hug.

"You did good." He said with a trace of disappointment in his voice.

I pulled away from him. "And you're a good loser." I teased.

He chuckled. "I wasn't expecting you to win, to be completely honest."

"I guess I'm just good at it." I smiled.

We played another round, and this time he won. Before I knew it, all of the guys wanted to play me; they wanted to see if they could beat me. Alex was the only one who hadn't played me, and when I asked him, he said no. Caleb said it was normal; Alex was usually on the side, observing everybody.

I told Caleb I was going to take a break; I wanted a chance to talk to Alex. I wasn't sure how successful I would be, but I wanted to give it a shot anyway. I sat down next to Alex on one of the couches, and nudged him with my arm.

"Hey." I said with a smile.

"Hi." He replied back. He looked scared, and his voice was quiet.

"So, how do you like it here?" I was trying to make small talk, even though I usually hated small talk.

"It's okay, I guess. I don't know how fun a mental hospital can be." He said nervously. He was looking all around the room, as if trying to find a way out.

I decided to talk about something…positive; if that were possible. "Do you want to play a game of pool?" I asked cheerfully.

He looked at me, his eyes wide. "No, thank you. I don't like pool much."

"Well, do you want to go to the green room and talk, where there are not so many people?"

He shook his head. "No, I think I'm going to go back to my room, actually." He got up and went to find his escort, leaving me alone on the couch.

Caleb came over and sat down next to me. "Unsuccessful? Don't feel bad. He doesn't really talk to anyone. Can you blame him though? Been bullied all his life, I would be the same way." He looked sadly over at Alex, who was now leaving with his escort.

Caleb's statement made me think of something I hadn't thought of before. "Why are you here Caleb?" I asked.

He laughed. "I'm not telling you that yet. Not a lot of people know why actually."

I frowned at him, and didn't bother questioning him further. I knew it would be futile. Instead I just looked around the room. It was raining outside right now, and the sky was growing darker. A storm was coming in. I liked storms though, they were relaxing to listen to and cool to watch. I turned and looked at Caleb.

"Hey, do you want to go sit in the green room? It's going to start storming, and I like watching them." I asked him.

"Sure." He said with a smile. We both got up and walked into the green room and pulled two chairs in front of the big window. We were just in time as I heard the first clap of thunder. We talked the entire time, and watching the storm. We talked about little things though; nothing to do with why we were here. I liked talking to him. He was a good listener and he laughed and said "mmhmm" at appropriate times in my stories.

It was getting close to dinner time when the storm was letting up. Caleb stood and extended his hand to me, I grabbed it. We went back into the green room and I found Gemma.

"How was your session today?" she asked, giving me a brief hug.

I shrugged. "I don't really want to talk about it. How was yours?"

"It was good actually. I feel good today." She smiled brightly.

"I'm glad. We should probably get going to dinner. It's almost seven." I said as I linked my arm with hers. Caleb was right beside us.

After dinner, Gemma and I returned to our room and decided to paint each other's nails. I never did stuff like this with Leah, and I never connected with any of the other girls very well. It was nice. Gemma was painting my nails a deep purple. She told me that she usually has "good days" and "bad days" that she and her therapist discuss during their sessions. Today, she was having a good day apparently.

"Gemma." I mumbled. She looked up at me with a puzzled expression on her face.

"I'm glad you're my roommate…and my friend." I added.

She beamed at me and gave me a quick hug. "I'm glad we're friends too, Emily." Her eyes were swelling with tears, and her cheeks had turned slightly pink.

"My dance instructor used to rape me…" I whispered so softly I wasn't sure if it was audible.

Gemma nearly dropped the brush to the nail polish. "Emily…" she said breathlessly. "We don't have to talk about this, you know." She put the nail polish down, and sat next to me on my bed, our backs to the wall.

My head was in her lap as I spoke. "It started off as him kissing me. At first I didn't mind it, you know? I had a bit of a crush on him. He kissed me in his office every week. Then eventually, he told me loved me. A couple weeks later were when he raped me. Do you want to know the most fucked up part about it?" I asked her angrily.

"What Emily?" she whispered.

"I fell in love with him. He raped me very week almost, and I fell in love with him. I didn't want to have sex with him, but I loved him. Isn't that the most confusing thing you've ever heard? When I was in the hospital, I called him for comfort. I wanted to go back home to him. I wanted to see him again." I said with disgust. I was seeing all of this more clearly, and I was beginning to hate myself.

Gemma sighed. "We can't choose who we love, Emily. It was messed up what he did to you, he's a psycho, and you have to let him go." She said firmly.

I sniffled; I had started to cry, but Gemma was wiping away my tears as they fell. "That's in your past now, Emily. Focus on now and every day after it. That's what matters now." She said to me softly. She would make a great mother someday, I thought to myself.

I told Gemma I was tired and wanted to go to bed. She nodded and before she hopped off my bed she said, "Thanks for telling me, Emily. It really does mean a lot." She smiled, shut off the light and went over to her bed, crawling underneath her covers.

I got under my own covers and rolled over. I felt a little better after telling Gemma, truthfully. I thought of earlier that day, sitting in the green room with Caleb, and trying to get Alex to talk more. I smiled to myself. Gemma was right; it was about the now.

I don't know what time it was but I woke up screaming and covered in sweat. Gemma was shaking me, and the light was shining in my eyes. A nurse was standing beside Gemma. I blinked, trying to focus, panting. I sat up and Gemma sat down next to me.

"Are you okay?" she asked nervously. The nurse was feeling my forehead and wiping my face with a cold wash cloth. My heart race was slowing, and so was my breathing.

"I had a nightmare." I said hoarsely. Darren was in it. He had trapped me in his office, and he was inside me again. I could feel his body heat in my dream, and his eyes were now haunting.

"It was just a dream, sweetheart. It's not real." Gemma said soothingly, stroking my hair away from my face. The nurse was taking my temperature, just to make sure I didn't have a fever, and fetched me a glass of cold water. She made sure I was calm before she left.

"Gemma, it was about Darren. It was real." I said with a trace of annoyance in my voice, but regretted it quickly, remembering Gemma couldn't read my mind.

She nodded. "Well, that's all done and over with Emily. He can't hurt you anymore." She was so forgiving of my attitude. She helped me get settled into bed again, and stopped midway to turn off the light.

"I have an idea!" she said cheerfully.

"Hmm?" I was dozing off again and I wanted nothing more than to close my eyes and sleep.

I heard a loud, scraping noise and looked in Gemma's direction. She was pushing her bed next to mine, so our beds were practically touching.

"This way, if you have a nightmare, I'll be right here to wake you up." She said happily. "Now go back to sleep!" she demanded as she turned off the light.

I laughed to myself at Gemma's ability to change tone so quickly, and snuggled back down in my blankets. I thought of Caleb this time before drifting off to sleep, and I slept peacefully through the rest of the night.

At Group the next day we talked about things we like about ourselves, things we like about others around us. Apparently, self-esteem was in issue for some people, me included. Anna still remained somewhat silent, she couldn't think of anything that she liked about herself. Alex, however, gave an unexpected response.

"I like how Emily tried talking to me the other night." He had said. I was shocked, and I gave him a small smile. Everyone else seemed pleased as well.

Friday past quickly, my session with Dr. John was spent discussing how I was adjusting to the place and admiring the progress I was making already. He seemed to be pleased at the fact that I was eating at least a little bit of my meals each day. I felt proud of myself, and I liked feeling proud of myself.

The evening was uneventful. I spent it in the rec room like I did almost every night with Gemma and Caleb, and Alex was starting to become part of our little group. Gemma and I didn't talk much when we got back to our room; we both just crawled into bed and fell asleep almost immediately.

Saturday, I had my first art class. I was nervous because I didn't know what to expect and never was good at art in school. I didn't want to embarrass myself. I was nervous that

whole morning, and barely touched any of my omelet. Breakfast seemed to pass by quickly this morning, and I had a little bit of time to myself before I had to go to art. I decided I would ask Gemma about the art class, and see if I had anything to worry about.

We were back in our room and I finally spoke up and asked, "Gemma, what's the art class like? Do you know?"

She got a serious look on her face, and stared at me intently. "The teacher is a total hard ass. I was so glad when I didn't have to take art anymore. It was the worst experience of my life." She said darkly.

I groaned. "Great."

"Gemma, I'm kidding." She chuckled. "Art class is a joke, and the teacher, she's a sweetheart. You'll be fine. We're in a mental hospital, not an art school." She nudged my arm playfully and laughed again.

The rest of our hour passed by quickly, and Caleb was right on time to escort me to art. I told him what Gemma said and he laughed. "That's Gemma. But she's right, you have nothing to be nervous about. You just sit around and paint your feelings. That's what Ms. Barns tells you to do anyway." He said lightly. He told me he would be back to pick me up, and we said good bye.

I walked into the room and finally saw the source of the tacky pictures that covered the walls of the building. I saw what Caleb meant about "painting our feelings." There was an old woman standing in the front of the room, bending down to clean something up off the floor. The room was filled with several circle tables, and the counters were lined with paint bottles, containers of paint brushes and pallets. Paper of all colors and sizes were stacked on another counter, and finally a full counter with sinks. Smocks were on a rack over by a door leading to the outside, which lead to the courtyard. There were plenty of windows, letting the sun light up the room. The paint fumes were somewhat overwhelming though. The lady finally stood up and had a handful of red paper towels.

Her hair was the same color as the red paint on the paper towels, her eyes were a bright, sky blue, and her cheeks were rosy. She was short and stumpy; I felt like I was looking at a younger version of Mrs. Clause.

"Well hello darlin'!" her southern accent was pretty thick.

"Erm, hi." I said awkwardly. I was still standing by the door and realized I was getting in the way; kids were starting to come into the room. Some gave me annoyed looks as they pushed past me. I walked up to the desk.

"I'm new here." I said. "This is my first art class."

Her face spread into a wide smile. "Oh yes! Emily, right? I'm Ms. Barns! Welcome, welcome!"

I smiled back and muttered "Thank you."

She threw away the paper towels, and directed me over to a table, with only one other person at it; Anna. I smiled to myself. Finally, I would have an opportunity and reason to talk to her. She only mutters a word or two during meals, and freezes up during group. I sat down across from her, giving us each half of the table. I looked at her and smiled, and to my surprise, she smiled back. Our attention was turned to Ms. Barns though as she began to speak.

"Ok, y'all, we have a new member with us today! Her name is Emily. So everybody make her feel welcome." She gave the rest of the kids a stern stare. I didn't recognize many of them. I thought some of them might be in group with me, but I wasn't completely sure. "Now, today, we're going to be painting something that makes you happy! So think happy thoughts!" she said happily, and clapped her hands together. She walked back to her desk, and turned to her computer.

Anna and I both got up and went to get paper, paint brushes and the rest of our supplies. I already knew what I was going to paint. Anna moved slowly, and tentatively, I had noticed. She seemed so fragile. She wasn't exactly skinny like me, but she was definitely not average weight for her age. She sat back down at the table, and pushed her platinum blonde hair into a pony tail. She began pouring different color paints onto the pallet, and I could tell she was lost in thought. I wasn't going to bother her right now.

I began mixing my own colors together, and dipped the paintbrush in the paint. I stared at my paper and decided how I wanted to approach this. I shrugged, and closed my eyes. I recalled the most common piece of music we listen to during dance, and began to move the brush across the paper as I felt the music coursing back to my bones. I can't describe what it felt like, a tingly feeling maybe. I don't really know. I didn't even look at what colors I was dipping my paint brush in, I just kept my eyes closed. Finally, when the song ended in my head and opened my eyes. Anna was staring at me, and so was Ms. Barns, who was now standing over my shoulder. When did she get there?

"Emily," she breathed. "This is fantastic!"

I blushed. "Oh, um, thank you. I didn't really try, I just-"

"Well, whatever you did, it turned out beautifully!" she said excitedly. She laid the paper down in front of me, so I could actually look at my own art work.

She was right, it was beautiful. The different colors were painted in graceful patterns across the paper, crossing every once in a while, and the colors swirled together. I smiled. I was impressed with myself. I looked up and Anna was still staring at me. Her paper was

still blank, and her pallet was untouched. I looked away quickly, and started cleaning up my station. The hour was almost over, and I didn't want to make Caleb wait.

Noon came, and Ms. Barns said she would see us next week. I took my painting with me. I was walking to the door when I heard a faint voice behind me.

"Hey, Emily."

I turned around, and it was Anna.

"Y-yes?" I stammered, shocked that she spoke to me.

"You're a good artist." She said quietly. She strode past me, and out the door.

I stood rooted on the post, confused. I shook my head and walked out the door to Caleb leaning up against the wall.

"Hey." He said with a smile.

"Hi." I smiled back. We started walking. The silence between us had become comfortable, and I enjoyed being able to explore my thoughts with him by my side. We were half way to lunch when he said, "Can I see what you made in art?" he smiled shyly, and knew he probably shouldn't have asked.

"I don't really want to share it with people. I mean Ms. Barns saw it, but she kind of just took it from me." I blushed and looked away. I felt silly for not letting him see my painting, but I just didn't want to share it, not this one at least, not even with Gemma. I wanted this to be something for my eyes only now. "I'm sorry." I said, and truly I was.

He shook his head, and looked at me. "It's okay. I understand." I could tell that he did. "I bet it's beautiful though." He said so quietly, I could barely hear him. It made me blush more.

We got to the cafeteria, and I went to my table with Gemma and the rest of the girls. It was pizza and salad for lunch. I could handle some of the salad, and maybe a bite or two of pizza; possibly. We talked about little things over lunch and Anna actually spoke once or twice, but nothing more than a couple of words.

We had the rest of the day to ourselves and the girls wanted to do a movie marathon in the rec room. Gemma and I agreed to go. Caleb didn't want to stay though, so he dropped me off and left. Gemma and I claimed a love seat for ourselves, and put pillows in our laps. One of the girls had popped in The Notebook and Gemma and I silently agreed to not pay attention to this particular movie.

"So, tomorrow's visitor's day." She said awkwardly.

"I know. I have no clue if my mom is coming or not. I'm kind of hoping she doesn't, to be honest." I said, leaning against the back of the couch and placing my hand on my head.

Gemma nodded, and I could tell she hadn't really heard me. "I would love it if my mom would come." She whispered. Everyone else was watching the movie, so it was almost impossible to talk.

"Has she not visited you yet?" I asked.

"No. She used to just sit there while my dad would beat me. I knew she could hear me scream and cry, but she never did anything. I suppose now she feels ashamed, and guilty, as she should, but she's my mom, and I want to see her." Gemma said, wiping away a tear from her cheek.

I reached my hand out and put it on her knee. "Gem, your mom will come when she's ready. Trust me. You are her daughter, and she loves you no matter what. She will visit you." I said reassuringly.

Gemma smiled at me, "Thanks, Em. So, do you think we'll have any visitors tomorrow?" she asked lightly.

"Well, Darren wouldn't be allowed to. My mom might, but when I left the hospital I was mad at her, so maybe not. My friend Leah hasn't tried talking to me since she called me in the hospital once. So as for me, probably not. You, I think it's possible." I grinned aat her.

We turned our attention to the rest of The Notebook, then joined in the laughter while watching Bridesmaids, and before we knew it, it was close to dinner time. Caleb came back to escort me, and Gemma joined us in our walk to the cafeteria.

I ate some of my dinner that night, but not much. Gemma and I just sat around our room for the night. We didn't feel like being around the other girls, but it was too cool outside tonight to sit in the courtyard or green room. I fell asleep early that night, and slept peacefully.

I woke up the next morning, and got showered and dressed, then went down to breakfast, escorted by Caleb of course. I wasn't very hungry to begin with, and I was nervous about visitor's day. I didn't even know if anyone was coming. I hadn't heard anything while I'd been here. Gemma tried telling me it's no big deal if you don't have a visitor, most kids didn't, but it didn't make me feel any better.

Soon rolled around, and it was time to see who my visitor was. Caleb escorted me to the lounge room, made for visits, and I opened the door, and my jaw dropped to the floor.

My breathing started to quicken, my heart was starting to race, and my mouth was going dry. I don't think I was happy to see him. His dark blue eyes sparkling mischievously, and his smirk that he permanently wore. He was leaned back against the couch, he arms draped over the back of the couch. He looked over at me, and stood to greet me.

No, no, no. This wasn't possible! He wasn't allowed here! How was he here? I backed up against the wall as he walked closer to me.

"Hello darling." He said softly, now inches away from me.

"What are you doing here?" I blurted.

He cocked his head to the side. "Not happy to see me? I went through a lot of trouble to be here Emily. We haven't spoken since that day you called me from the hospital." He said. His face was centimeters from mine, and I could feel his hot breath on my face.

"I'm not allowed to talk to you. And I realized since then that we used to have is wrong. It shouldn't have happened." I tried to say firmly, but my voice was faltering.

Darren was running his hand through my hair, and staring into my eyes with such intensity it was making me nervous. Then, he smirked.

"Are you talking about this?" he asked slyly.

I didn't have time to answer before his lips were against mine, and his tongue was trying to find his way into my mouth, but I wouldn't let him. I pushed my hands against his chest, hoping to push him off of me, but it was to no avail. He was too strong for me. I started to cry, realizing how completely helpless I was. Darren had me pinned against the wall, and any resistance just made him grip me harder. I wasn't even kissing him back, but he still kept persisting. His hands were traveling down my back, to my bottom, and around to my front. He was just working the zipper of my pants when the door burst open and a male's voice cried "Get away from her!"

I don't know what made Darren back away so quickly because I fell to the floor as soon as he let me go, and let the tears flow. I was choking on my sobs, and crying so loudly, I couldn't hear what was going on with Darren. I felt firm, warm, strong arms around me, and at first I resisted, but then I realized they had a different purpose. The arms wrapped around me, and I cried into the person's chest. It was only when my crying slowed, that I looked up to see who was cradling me. It was Caleb.

Dr. John was sitting on the couch, filling out papers. He looked furious, and was writing faster than I had ever seen him write in his office. I realized it was he who came bursting through the door, and Caleb must have been nearby.

"Thanks." I mumbled to Caleb, stroking his arm as I stood up. He helped me up and I walked over to the couch where Dr. John was seated.

"Dr. John. I didn't arrange or ask Darren to come. I didn't want him to be here." I said, my voice shaking.

He took a deep breath before speaking. "I know, Emily. I know you had nothing to do with it. Our security team is being reprimanded for this, and security will be increased from now on. We can't have this happening to you, or anyone else. We still don't know how he managed to get in yet, but I have to talk with the front desk." His was gentle, and I was glad he knew this was nothing involving me.

"Should I leave you alone now?" I asked.

"For now, yes. I will check up on you this evening to make sure you're okay. Then I see you tomorrow, so we will talk then as well." He smiled at me, but I could tell it was forced. I nodded.

"Caleb." Dr. John called out. "Escort Emily to the nurse and have her checked over to make sure there are no physical injuries, please."

"Will do Sir." Caleb replied. We joined arms and walked out of the room.

I told the nurse I only felt slightly dizzy and nauseous, so she gave me some tums and told me to just rest for the rest of the day, and to drink plenty of water. The shock would wear off as long as I was resting. I nodded, I couldn't completely focus, I just wanted to get back to my room and lay down and forget about today.

Caleb joined arms with me again and led me down the path to my room. He didn't try to talk to me and I was glad that he didn't. I had a feeling he knew that I just wanted to go to my room. We reached my room and he helped me lay down and kissed me on the cheek before he left. The kiss shocked me, but I smiled as he walked out of the door. I didn't bother getting under my covers or anything, I just rolled over and closed my eyes, thinking of anything but Darren.

I woke up hours later, and felt disoriented. It took me a couple of seconds to remember that I was in my bed. My dreams were unsettling, and weird, but Darren wasn't in them. I didn't have the desire to move so I just curled up in a ball and faced my wall. All I could think about was Darren. How did he manage to show up? I would have thought they would have stopped him. I could remember how his body felt against mine; heavy and uncomfortable. He was sweaty, and I could smell his cologne on my clothes; too musky. I shook my head, trying to eliminate thoughts of him. I decided that I needed to get up and do something, or else thoughts of him were just going to keep coming back. I got out of the bed and wondered how I was going to get Darren to come and get me. I decided not to put too much thought in to it, and just started walking down to the rec room. No one stopped me, and no one was even in the hallway. I walked into the room and saw Gemma over by Anna and Leila. I decided to walk over to them, and when I approached, Gemma turned and gave me a worried look.

"I heard what happened. Are you okay?" she asked, sitting me down in a chair.

"I guess. I'm just out of it." I said blankly.

Leila and Anna got the hint that they should leave us alone, and so they went into the green room. They gave me small smiles and mumbled "feel better." I smiled back as thanks.

Gemma sat down in front of me, and looked me in the eyes. "Emily, are you sure you're okay?"

I nodded. "I really just want to forget about it, to be honest. I don't want to talk about it, okay?" I said.

"Okay." She agreed, but I could tell she wanted to badger with me questions about it. I didn't want to answer questions about Darren. I wanted to be around people, but I didn't want to talk.

We sat in silence for a while, watching T.V. I couldn't tell you what was on that night, because I hadn't really been paying attention. I couldn't forget about the incident today. I felt disgusting, and filthy, and empty, like I used to. I couldn't help it, but tears started forming in my eyes, and I tried blinking them back. I cried silently for a couple minutes; the tears rolling down my cheeks, and my nose running, until Gemma turned to look at me, and noticed.

"Oh, sweetie, no. Don't cry. Talk to me." She grabbed both my hands with one of hers, and began wiping my tears.

I sniffled. "Can you just ask Caleb to take me Dr. John?" I asked, my voice cracking. I was trying not to let out a sob, but the tears were choking me at this point.

Gemma didn't question me, she just nodded and went to find Darren. He came over in less than a minute, and we left the rec room and started our walk to Dr. John's office. I was trying to hold in my sobs but I couldn't do it any longer. I let out a sob in between my shallow breaths, and Caleb turned to look at me. He pulled me over to a bench, and sat down next to me, putting his arm around me. I didn't care that we were in the hallway, and people would probably see me cry; I leaned in to him, and let it out.

His grip on me had gotten tighter, the harder I cried, and his hand was stroking up and down my arm. He didn't say anything, he just let me cry. I don't know how long we stayed like that for, but when I was finally done crying I looked up at him and said, "I'm okay now."

He wiped away tears still on my cheeks, and looked at me with concern written all over. "Are you sure?"

I nodded. "Yeah."

We stood up and walked the rest of the way to Dr. John's office. He told me to just have Dr. John page him when I was done.

"Thank you." I said looking down at my feet, feeling slightly embarrassed.

Caleb smiled, and mumbled "Don't mention it." He waved as he walked off.

I walked into Dr. John's office and sat down at my normal spot. He looked up from his desk, and didn't question why I was here.

"Emily, I know that it's not your fault. We figured out how he got in, and we've made arrangements to make sure it doesn't happen again." He said firmly, rubbing his eyes.

"I don't really want to know how he got in, to be honest. I just…I want to know that I'm safe now." I said, my voice slightly shaky.

"You are safe, yes. But I talked with your group leader, and you're permitted to miss group this week to meet with me, so we can talk more in depth about this. Especially what happened today."

"But that's so unfair! I actually like group and-" I stopped myself. "No, you're right. Meeting with you every day this week would help." I sighed. I wanted to argue him on this but the truth is, I knew he was right, and besides, I was just the patient. There was nothing I could do to change this.

For the rest of the time that I spent in his office, we talked about making myself start to believe that I was safe, and wouldn't be seeing Darren again. I certainly felt better than I did before I came to him earlier in the day.

Caleb was waiting outside for me and he told me it was close to dinner time by now. We just went straight to the cafeteria and sat at a table.

"So, how are you feeling now?" he sounded hesitant in asking me, and he was wringing his hands.

I shrugged. "I feel better than I did earlier today. I'm definitely less scared, and I don't feel so vulnerable."

He nodded and his jaw was clenched. "You know, I've never seen anything like what I saw today, in my lifetime. I know you're the one it actually happened to, but watching it was just so…scary. I wanted to hit the guy, but Dr. John wouldn't let me…" his voice trailed off.

I was speechless for a second mainly because I couldn't tell what Caleb was trying to say.

"Uhm…uhh…are you-?" I started to say, but he cut me off.

"I care about you a lot. I've come to realize that. I feel the need to be protective over you, and to be honest, I feel angry with myself because I couldn't go in there and help you today." I could hear the anger in his voice, and my heart ached for him.

This wasn't his fault, and he shouldn't have felt bad for not being able to help. "Caleb, it's okay. I'm not mad at anyone, well, except maybe security, but, I'm not mad at you or anyone else. So don't be mad at yourself, okay? I'm alive, and uninjured." I said reassuringly, placing my hand on his arm.

He looked down at my hand, and placed his on top briefly. "Well, luckily, that's not going to happen again, so we don't have to worry about it anymore." He tried to give me a reassuring smile, but I could tell he didn't even believe himself.

I barely touched my dinner. I felt disgusting today, and I didn't feel like making myself feel worse. Gemma didn't bother bugging me about it, either. I finished eating, the food barely touched, and told Gemma I would see her back in the room later. She knew better than to argue, and just nodded. I went over to Caleb's table, and asked him to take me back when he was done eating. He agreed, and ten minutes later we left the cafeteria, and I was back in my room by seven thirty.

I didn't think I had any tears left in me, but I was wrong apparently. I curled up in a ball on my bed, hugging my pillow and let the tears fall. My heart felt heavy, and I felt like I was going to be sick. I could feel all of my stress, sadness and anger pouring out of me. My sobs were those loud, obnoxious kinds. I couldn't help it though, they were uncontrollable. I thought about Darren, and how unfair it was that he could take control of me that easily. I was so angry with myself too, for letting that happen. God, I hated myself. I didn't care that it was against the rules for me, I went over the window and opened it and stuck my torso out. I threw up what little I ate today into the grass and closed the window again. I sat back down on my bed, wiping my eyes and sniffling. Right after I threw up, I knew that I was right back where I started.

Chapter 6

A month had passed since that day that Darren visited me. Since then, I hadn't been allowed any visitors, the hospital was really taking their time making sure no visitors that weren't allowed, couldn't get in. I was thankful for this though.

Gemma and I had talked the day after it happened, and I apologized for pushing away. She said she understood though, she would have been the same way. Caleb and I have become a lot closer, but I'm not sure if he likes me or not. I finally admitted to myself that I like him; I like him a lot. I haven't told anyone this though. I'll tell Gemma when I'm ready.

Art class is my favorite thing to do throughout the week. I look forward to Saturdays now, and Ms. Barns loves my art work. She tells me every week that I should make it a side career in my future. Everyone seems annoyed with me though, I would be too if I saw Ms. Barns going on and on about a student. Anna talked to me a couple of times, but nothing too personal. They were always things about the other kids here, or how our days have been, little things like that. She was warming up to me, I could tell.

My sessions with Dr. John have really been progressing. I realized that I never did truly love Darren, and he didn't truly love me. The next thing we're working on is my actual weight issue. I still feel fat most days, but I have been eating about 1/3 of my meals now. Dr. John says I'm slowly, but surely getting better. I have a session with him today actually.

I also got enough gold stars to be able to escort myself to meals and the rec room. Caleb still comes with me sometimes though; it's what we were used to by now. Caleb, Gemma and I walked down to breakfast together and sat a table away from everyone else. Gemma and I still talked to the other girls, but once this new girl Isabel had come, the table has been filled with drama. Gemma and Caleb had become good friends, so our trio worked out. I ate about half of my pancake (they were small pancakes), a couple bites of my scrambled eggs and one whole strip of bacon. Gemma and Caleb always told me how well I was doing, and encouraged me to try and eat a bit more. Sometimes I listened to them; sometimes I still didn't believe them.

I went through my day as I normally did. I had breakfast with Gemma and Caleb, and then we went for a walk among the grounds and sat by the pond. Then we had lunch together, and before I knew it, it was time for my session with Dr. John. I waved good-bye as I headed towards his office, and Gemma and Caleb set off towards the rec room. I greeted Dr. John with a smile, and sat down on my usual spot of the couch.

"So," he began in an airy tone. "I've been thinking about our meetings, and I think I came up with an idea that will keep up with your progression."

"Oh really?" I inquired.

His face spread into a smile and the corners of his mouth almost touched his eyes. "Oh yes. I think it would be wise if you focus on the future. Not the past, not the present, but the future. What can you do to make your future better from your past? That's what I want to start focusing on. We can brainstorm ideas together, and see what we come up with. Sound good?"

I nodded. I truly did like the idea. I think it would help me get better quicker, and that's what I was after, wasn't it? "Sure, sounds good!" I exclaimed enthusiastically. I returned his smile.

"Also, I have a piece of news for you that might make this process a bit easier for you to begin." Dr. John stated, the smiling still not fading. Something seriously good had happened.

I looked at him quizzically.

"I received confirmation today that Darren starts his sentence in jail tomorrow. He got 15 years. It was originally 10 years, but I got 5 added on once they found out you were in a severe mental and physical condition because of it. I didn't want to tell you any of this while he was still in trial, because I didn't want to get your hopes up." He said this all very fast, and it took me a couple of seconds to understand what he was telling me.

"So…I don't have to worry about Darren harming me anymore?!" I screeched. I could feel my heart beat picking up, and a smile spread on my face. This was amazing! This feeling was euphoric! I wouldn't have to worry about Darren for the next fifteen years!

Dr. John shook his head. "That's right Emily. From now on, Darren will not be in your future. So! Let's get down to business!" he clapped his hands together and sat down at his desk.

I relished in the excitement of the news for just one more moment before turning my attention to Dr. John. I would have plenty of time to think about this and accept this later.

"I want to ask you, Emily, a question that will start off our new idea." He put on his glasses, and retrieved a pen and notebook from his drawer. "Close your eyes, and picture your life in five years. What do you see?"

I did as I was told. I closed my eyes, but to my disappointment, saw nothing. Black. Darkness. "I don't see anything." I said flatly.

"Think. Take some time. You've been out of treatment for a long time now, you're back on your feet. Where are you living? Are you seeing anyone?" I could hear his soft voice floating to my ears as I thought about his questions and tried so hard to see something.

I waited and suddenly, it was like my brain clicked back on. "I see New York City. I want to leave this town and move to New York." I whispered. "Gemma's with me too." I could actually see it. The skyscrapers. Times Square. Gemma's bright, smiling face looking over at me. I don't know why we're there. I opened my eyes with the biggest smile on my face. I had something to work towards.

Right after my session, I ran to tell Gemma and Caleb about Darren. They were just as excited as I was, if not more. Caleb picked me up and spun me around, while Gemma wiped a tear from her eye. We ran to tell the rest of our friends, and we managed to have a small celebration.

I was standing with Gemma, laughing at something one of the boys had said, when I felt a tap on my shoulder. I turned around to see Alex standing behind me.

"Oh, hey!" I exclaimed, glad to see that Alex had approached me. "What's up?"

Alex pulled me in for an unexpected hug and said, "I'm glad he's in jail." I squeezed him back and whispered, "So am I."

Alex let go and I gave him a smile. "Want to join the celebration?" I asked. He nodded and came over to join our small group. Tonight was the first time I saw Alex engage in a social activity willingly and it brought tears of joy to my eyes.

The next day at group, I learned not everyone was ecstatic about Darren being put away. Isabel had no problem saying that she could care less that Darren was locked up. It had started an argument between Isabel and Gemma, and soon everyone was chiming in. Lisa, our group leader, finally chimed in and told everyone to knock it off.

"Isabel, in group, we support everyone. Not tear them down." Lisa scolded.

Isabel crossed her arms across her chest and said indignantly, "I just don't think it's fair that other people's rapists are put away and they don't get a party thrown for them. That's all. Why should Emily be special?" She glared right at me as she spoke.

Gemma was about to speak again but I cut her off. "Isabel, I'm sorry if you're jealous that a party wasn't thrown for you. Being a rape victim sucks, we both know that. But it's neither my fault nor my problem that you didn't tell your friends like I told mine. That's why they threw me a party, because I had friends I could trust, and who support me. Maybe if you stopped being such a bitch all the time, you'd have people to support you too. I'm sure a lot of us would love to support you in your recovery, but it's kind of hard to when you stomp around bursting people's bubbles every day." I somehow managed to keep my tone calm and level, but inside I was boiling. Isabel had no right to knock me down on my good news.

Isabel continued to glare at me until she finally stood up and stalked out of the room, slamming the door behind her. I nervously looked at Lisa, who nodded, signaling I could go after her. I nodded back and left the room. I heard a faint sobbing sound and followed it down the hall way to the green room, where I could see Isabel crying on a couch. I slowly approached, waiting to see if she noticed me; she didn't. Her black hair was up in a sloppy bun, and her olive skin was glowing from the sunlight. She really was pretty, it was just hard to recognize because of her horrible personality.

"Isabel?" I asked as I walked over to her. She turned to face me, her gray eyes shining with tears.

"I don't want your sympathy." Her tone was harsh and cold.

I sighed. "Really? Because if you didn't, you wouldn't have thrown a fit all day." I said sarcastically, but regretting it immediately. I was here to make amends, not continue the fight. "I'm sorry…"

She looked at me again and I could see the hurt in her eyes. "You're not special just because everyone pays attention to you and people throw you parties."

"Trust me…I know that. I never once said I was special. I don't think I'm special. It's just that I've been waiting for a long time for Darren to be put away, and it finally happened. It's a relief. A huge relief. I feel like I can breathe again." I said calmly, sitting down next to her.

She sniffled and reached for a tissue. "Yeah well, when my step-brother was put away, do you know what I got? Hate mail. His friends said I should have kept my mouth shut. My step-dad refuses to believe it this day. Even some of my friends from home think I made it up. Nobody celebrated with me when that bastard was finally out of my life. Not a single person. I didn't expect here to be any different." She looked out the window the entire time that she spoke, and I could hear her voice catch in her throat a couple of times.

"Isabel…you're in a mental hospital now. Everybody knows pain. There would have been at least one person who would have understood what you went through. It's not like back home." I spoke in a gentle voice, and I reached out to touch her arm but she retreated.

"I didn't think about it! God, see, I'm even being blamed for not thinking straight." More tears spilled out of her eyes and she wiped them away as quickly as she could.

I felt bad for her, I really did. I understood perfectly what it was like to be so traumatized, you don't think right for a long period of time.

"Look, you want people to understand you, to know that you are not in the wrong in your situation, to be your friend. But keep acting the way you have and you're not going to get any of that. Try being nice to people, it actually gets you somewhere." I said condescendingly. I got up off the couch, handed Isabel another tissue and went back to group.

The rest of the session was peaceful as Isabel didn't return. But Lisa wanted us to talk about other things besides my rapist's lock up. Alex spoke voluntarily, which was a pleasant surprise for everyone. Though the biggest surprise was that Caleb told us all a little bit about why he was here; that part I listened to very intently.

"I was about twelve at the time, and my dad had died the year before. So I was the new man of the house, you know? My sister was only eight, and my mom was stuck in a depression and constantly in danger of losing her low-wage job. I felt like it was my responsibility to take care of my family. So I began…"

But we didn't find out what Caleb began doing because Lisa announced that time was up. I ran to catch up with Caleb but as soon as I approached him he said, "Don't even think about it, Emily. I'm not talking about it outside of group." I decided it was best not to press him.

The rest of the week passed by smoothly. Everyone had noticed that Isabel was a bit more friendly after our little fight on Tuesday. Dr. John and I discussed my dream to continue dancing and go to college for dancing in New York. He said that I needed to be healthy if I wanted to do that, and if that's what it took, I was willing to try.

I was really looking forward to Sunday because my mom was coming to visit, and it was the first time I was allowed visitors since Darren had gotten in. It was all I could talk about, and by Thursday, Gemma and Caleb were slightly annoyed with me, though they never said anything. They were good friends like that.

I really wanted to ask Caleb about his story, but I knew he wouldn't talk, so I kept my mouth shut. We didn't get a chance to hear the rest of it on Thursday because Lisa wanted us to think of five things we like about ourselves, and five things we like about another person. If we couldn't think of five things, other people were allowed to chime in. It was actually really nice to know that people were truly fond of each other; we were slowly becoming a family.

It was Gemma's turn to speak, and she was having difficulty coming up with things she liked about herself, so right away I chimed in, "Gemma's the best friend anyone could ever ask for." She looked over at me, and smiled. "Thank you," she mouthed.

Soon, other people were chipping in what they thought about Gemma.

"She's always says hi to me at breakfast!"

"She'll listen to you if you need someone to talk to."

The compliments kept going, and Gemma was nearly in tears by the end. Gemma had become my friend so quickly when I first got here, and I could legitimately say she I is one of my best friends now. I wanted to make it known to her that I'm not the only who thinks she is wonderful.

By the time group was over, everyone was in a great mood, having heard so many lovely things about themselves. Even Anna was smiling! Alex was talking to some of the guys in the group, which was a first. Gemma and Caleb didn't so annoyed with me anymore, as we linked arms and walked to dinner.

As I grabbed my hamburger, steak fries and water, I remembered what Dr. John said about needing to be healthy if I wanted to continue to dance. So that night at dinner, I ate half of my hamburger and had only four French fries left on my plate. Gemma, the rest of

the girls (including Isabel) clapped and whooped and hollered as I smiled, finally feeling somewhat okay with eating that much. I couldn't wait to tell Dr. John.

Two o'clock came rather quickly the next day, and for once, I was glad. I couldn't wait to tell Dr. John about dinner last night. He would be so proud. Even Caleb told me how proud he was of me on our way to Dr. John's office. I loved that Caleb still walked with me, though I no longer needed an escort to my appointments.

"I'll see you at three?" he asked, showing off his dazzling smile.

"Yep!" I said as I opened the door to Dr. John's office.

"Hellllo, Dr. John." I flopped down on the couch and placed a pillow on my lap.

"You seem to be in a good mood?" Dr. John asked quizzically, but happy all the same.

"I am! And I have something to tell you that will make you proud of me!"

"Do tell?" he grabbed his notepad and pen, ready to scribble down what I was about to say.

"I ate half of my hamburger and all but four of my French fries at dinner last night!" I exclaimed, clapping my hands together.

Dr. John smiled broadly, forgetting to write my news down. "Emily that is fantastic! You are doing so, so well! I am truly proud of you."

"Thanks." I smiled, and waited for what he had to say next.

"Your news is actually an excellent lead in for today's topic session." He said, returning to his normal self.

"What is it?"

"Well, it's been a little over a month since you first came here, and we should have discussed your first month's progress then, but with the Darren incident…it got delayed. So, that is what we are discussing today."

I nodded. "What does that include? My one month's progress?" I was scared that he had somehow found out about the two nights that I threw up my meals since I've been here.

"Well, it means we'll discuss your food intake. How you've adjusted to being here. Any improvement in therapy sessions. Things like that." He said simply.

"Okay." I was shaking, and slightly nervous. I didn't really want to remember how I used to be just one short month ago. I knew I had come such a long way.

"So, let's start with your food intake…let's see here…" he pulled out a chart, and examined it for a moment. His brow furrowing, before a smile split across his face for the second time this meeting. "Good news! You've increased your food intake, as I'm sure you already knew. How do you feel about eating now, Emily?"

I sighed and considered how to answer this question. "I'm not really sure. I definitely don't feel gross like I used to. I don't really feel it sit in my stomach as often as I used to. But I know I'm not ready to eat a full meal yet. That'd be too much."

Dr. John scribbled on his note pad and put the chart away. "How about your life here? Do you feel like you've adjusted okay?"

I thought back to how quickly and easily Gemma and I had become friends. I only knew her for a day when we started confiding in each other. It was if I had known her all my life. Then Caleb popped into my head; his pearly white teeth, and the tattoo on his wrist. The easy-going vibe he gave off, and how comfortable I had grown to be around him. Even Anna and Alex came into my mind. They were starting to grow on me, even if they didn't talk much still.

I smiled. "Yeah, I think I've adjusted quite well." I said quietly.

Dr. John nodded and made some more scribbles. "You've had a great deal of improvement since your very first therapy session, Emily. Do you remember your first therapy session?"

Of course I did. I was still in the hospital then, and I didn't want to be there. I spent the whole session crying, wishing I was back at home. I shuddered and pushed the thought back out.

"Yeah, I remember."

I left Dr. John's one hour later feeling slightly less happy, mainly because of all the memories our session brought back. Caleb could tell I didn't want to talk, and didn't press me to. I went back to my room and curled up on my bed. I needed to be alone with my thoughts for a little while.

It was crazy to think that my life had changed so suddenly that day that I collapsed in my basement. I thought nothing was wrong me with back then. I was so happy to be so skinny, so unhealthy. Then I did everything I could to not get better, and it nearly cost me my life. I spent so many hours crying; in my bed, in the shower, in Dr. John's office. I wasted so much time thinking about Darren, wanting to be back home with him. I was so stupid.

Then I was forced to come here. At first I didn't want to. I didn't think I needed help. Until I saw that the girls around me weren't skinny like me, but were still beautiful. That was when I knew that I had a problem. I remembered my first meal, panicking when I

thought I had to eat it all. Then the flood of relief when Dr. John told me I didn't. I remembered being scared of Caleb at first, and the way Gemma took me in that first day.

I remembered the night that I threw up in the shower and begged Caleb not to tell on me. And the day Caleb and I sat talking in the green room, watching the storm. He took care of me right away too. He carried me down hallways plenty of times, and still walked with me everywhere I went. I remembered admitting to myself that I like Caleb.

I really had changed in the month that I've been here, and I was actually quite shocked. I didn't have a panic attack every time meal time approached. I could eat without feeling so disgustingly fat afterwards; though some days I still hated how I looked. But I could tell I was starting to get better. I really was. I smiled as I truly realized for the first time; it's not the past that matters, nor the future, but the present. And right now, I was Emily, probably over ninety pounds, with friends who cared about me, and the will to get better. I could totally do this. I could recover and become a professional dancer.

Sunday quickly came, and I was beyond excited to see my mom. I felt bad for hanging up on her that day in the hospital, and the first thing I would do is apologize. She was actually supportive of me and my treatment and I shouldn't have treated her so poorly. Not to mention, she bringing more of my clothes and belongings. I was still annoyed that my room was more bare that Gemma's side. It didn't help that she commented on it at least once a week.

I ate one and a half pancakes, and a few bites of scrambled eggs. Then I spent the rest of the morning watching T.V., anxiously awaiting for noon to come. The boys were in the green room, smoking their after breakfast cigarettes. Some of the girls were curled up in chairs reading a book, others were in the green room with the boys. Gemma went back to the room as she wasn't feeling well. I didn't mind having this alone time though. It gave me time to plan out different scenarios of my mom's visit.

Noon was almost here and I told Caleb I didn't want him to walk with me. Mainly because I didn't want my mom to pester me about him, because that's exactly what she would do. I walked to the opposite end of the building to the lounge room reserved for guest visits. The last time I went here, an unexpected Darren was standing in there. I shook my head to rid the thought. No, he was in jail now. It's not possible. It's just your mom. I grabbed the handle and pushed open the door.

But it wasn't my mom standing in the room. It was a man; a tall, fair skinned, blonde haired man. His face was soft and his gray eyes twinkled with delight. My heart started to race, as I had no clue who this man was. Maybe I got the time wrong? Maybe this was someone else's guest?

"I'm sorry, sir. I think you're waiting for someone else." I said as I began to back up towards the door.

"Emily?" His voice was soft, but warm. Somehow I knew he wasn't going to hurt me.

"Y-yes?" How did he know my name?!

"It's me! It's your father!"

My eyes widened in disbelief. Dad?

Chapter 7

This man could not be my father. But then again, I don't remember what he looks like, so he very well could be. He looked nothing like me though. The blonde hair, the gray eyes…I had none of it. I realized I was staring at him with my mouth gaping open still; I shut it and narrowed my eyes into a glare.

"I don't believe you." I said firmly, placing my hands on my hips. This man was not going to come in and mess with my life like this. I wouldn't let him.

He sighed, and ran his hand through his hair in frustration. I could tell things weren't going the way he expected. "I'm your father. Your full name is Emily Rose Gerard. You were born May fifteen in nineteen ninety four and you weighed seven pounds and nine ounces. Your mother was in labor with you for almost a day; you were a stubborn baby from the day you were born. You-"

"Okay!" I yelled over him, cutting him off. "I guess…I believe you."

A stranger couldn't possibly know these things. I accepted that he was my father, but that did not mean I was ready to accept him into my life. He came to hug me, and I backed away.

"I said I believe that you're my father, but that doesn't mean I'm ready to forgive you!" I said, my voice starting to rise and tears forming in my eyes. "You can't just walk back into my life as though nothing ever happened!" The anger was boiling inside of me.

My father backed away and sat down on one of the couches in defeat already. "Emily…let me explain."

"No! You left me. Your own daughter. You didn't think I was important and so you left. I asked mom, even until this day why you left. Because my own father was too much of a coward to tell me himself, or better yet, to stick around. Thanks to you, I ended up here!" I was full blown shouting now and my face felt hot. Tears were welling in my eyes as I waved my arms around the room, showing where his absence in my life had gotten me.

Don't think…Don't think that because you show up sixteen years later, that everything is going to be okay. It's not. I can't forgive you that easily. You've caused me a lot of problems." I said, choking on my tears.

"Emily. Sit down, and please listen to me." His voice was firm, yet he was begging me at the same time. His eyes were shining with tears, and I could tell my words had really stung him. *Good.*

I hesitated, before sitting down on the couch next to him. He took a deep breath before he started speaking.

"You've been under the impression for the past sixteen years, that I left you and your mother. That I so easily abandoned my baby girl. My first and only child. But Emily, you've got it all wrong. It was your mother who left me when you turned two. She had found someone else, and ran away with him and took you with her. The three of us, you me and your mother used to live in Chicago, that's where you were born. We lived in a very nice apartment, and were so close to being able to buy a house. I came home from work one day, excited to tell your mom about a house I found, and all that was there was a note on the table."

James,

I'm finally leaving you for Cliff. He can provide more than you've ever been able to. I'm taking Emily with me; she deserves a better life than this. So do I. I'm not telling you where we're moving to, I don't want you interfering with our new life. I'm sorry.

"She didn't even sign the note…I tried tracking you guys down by looking at her credit card charges but there were none; she had used cash for everything. All of her belongings were gone. Your crib was gone, everything. I was alone and I had no idea where she had taken you. I tried calling Child Services but they couldn't do anything without a lead as to where you were. I've been trying ever since that day, Emily, to find you. But you can imagine how difficult it must have been. You literally could have been everywhere in the world."

"You're lying!" I don't know if I actually thought he was lying or if I just didn't want to believe that my mom had actually done that.

"I'm not, Emily. I'm not. What does your mother say when you ask about me? Something about how it doesn't matter? I left you and that's the important thing, am I right?" He had grabbed my hand, and was looking me straight in the eye.

"That's actually exactly what she's told me my entire life…" I whispered as I broke our gaze. My heart hurt, and my brain felt all jumbled. Tears stung my eyes again, and I sniffled. "But why…why would she do that?"

"Exactly what your mother wrote in that note. She wasn't getting the life she wanted quick enough, so she left. I was so close to getting us that house, Emily. So very close, but she never even gave me the chance." He sounded so sad, and broken. I couldn't believe my mother had done this to us.

"I believe you…dad." I added cautiously to the end of my sentence.

His face broke into a smile and he hugged me tight; he smelled like fire wood and musky cologne. I thought about asking him how he even found me, but decided it didn't matter. He was back, and we had sixteen years of catching up to do.

"James?!" A shrill voice called from the door way. We both broke apart to see my mother staring, open-mouthed, at both of us. "What are you doing here?! How did you find her?" She sounded completely shocked, and she seemed scared.

"Catherine." My father said harshly, his mouth forming a tight line.

I stood up, my hands in fists at my sides, shaking in fury. I walked slowly towards my mom, glaring at her. She was the liar; she was the one who ruined my life. She was partially to blame for my problems.

"How. Could. You?!" I screamed, flipping over an end table. She flinched, and shut her eyes.

"Emily, I-" she tried to talk, but I wasn't going to let her. She knew she had been caught. She knew the secret was out.

"NO!" I screeched. "You let me go all my life thinking dad was this horrible person who abandoned his family. When really, it was you! You lied to me for sixteen years! You thought I was better off in a nice house with a man who left you in the end, instead of in an apartment with a man who loved us both! How long did Cliff stick around, mom? Until I was about five right? All the men that you've dated, they've never stayed. You left the best damn thing that ever happened to us. I thought dad was to blame for me being here, but really, it was your fault. You took me away from a man who would have shown me love, respect, courage, independence. And instead, I find love in a sick bastard who never thought I was beautiful! And now look at me! In a mental hospital and still under 100 pounds! You thought you were doing us a favor sixteen years ago, but in reality, you fucked up my life." My breathing was heavy, and I could feel my heart pounding in my chest.

"Emily, I did that all to protect you! It was what was best for you, sweetheart…" she reached out to touch me but I smacked her hand away.

"Don't touch me!" I yelled. "And what exactly were you protecting me from? Hmm? Love? Protection? Security? Because none of the men you had around ever gave me that!" I was full blown crying now. I couldn't stop the tears.

"When I get out of here, I'm moving in with dad." I said looking her dead in the eye.

"You'll do no such thing!" she shrieked. Her face was red and her eyes were bulging.

"Actually, I will, and I can. I'm eighteen, I can choose where I go. I choose dad. He's been more honest with me in these twenty minutes than you have for the past sixteen years." My tone was harsh, but I didn't care.

My mom shook her head and wiped a tear from her eye. "Fine." She said quietly. "If that's what you want then." She turned around slowly and walked out the door. We could hear her cries all the way down the hall.

I turned to look at my dad who had the biggest smile on his face, and looked pleased at the daughter he didn't get a chance to raise. I went over to the couch and sat back down next to him. This is where I felt safe.

"Nicely done!" my dad high-fived me and I laughed. "So, how much longer are you going to be in here?"

"I have no idea to be honest. I've been making a lot of improvement and I've only been here for a month, so maybe in a few months."

He nodded. "Well, I have a pent house in New York City, if you'd like to come and stay with me when you get out?"

"I would love that!" New York City was the start of all my dreams!

"Hey dad?"

"Yes?"

"Can you come visit every Sunday? Or every other Sunday? The sooner we start catching up the better."

He laughed. I liked his laugh. "I can definitely do every Sunday."

"Great."

He stared at me for a moment before pulling me in for another hug. "I've missed you so much, Emily."

"I've missed you too Dad. I really have."

Caleb knocked on the door to tell us our hour was done. I didn't mind introducing my dad to Caleb, though Caleb certainly looked shocked to see my dad. My dad made me promise to work hard at getting better, and I told him I do every day. We hugged once more before he left.

"So…" Caleb said nervously, shoving his hands in his pockets. "That's your dad then? He's actually your dad?" He sounded so unsure, and honestly I couldn't blame him.

"I didn't believe it at first. But, we talked, and everything's good now." I said firmly, showing I was done talking about the subject. I didn't want to share what fully happened in that room, except with Dr. John.

Caleb nodded and he said, "Well, I'm glad things are falling in to place for you. I really am." He flashed his perfect smile at me, and butterflies erupted in my stomach. "How about a game of pool?"

"You read my mind." I said as I linked my arm through his.

"So how was visitors' day yesterday?" Dr. John asked as he took out his notepad and pen.

"It was interesting. I actually…uh…met my dad for the first time." I was kind of nervous about telling Dr. John because I didn't need him bursting my bubble about this whole situation.

"How did that go?" he asked.

"Well, at first I didn't believe him, you know? I didn't remember what he looked like because I hadn't seen him since I was two. But he proved it, and he told me the truth about what really happened when I was two."

"And what was the truth?"

I took a big sigh before I began talking. "Basically my mom lied to me for sixteen years. My dad didn't leave us, she left him and took me with her." I was still so sensitive about this that I started tearing.

"Wow, that's a pretty big secret to keep from your child for sixteen years. How did you react when you found out?" He handed me a tissue as he spoke.

"I freaked out. She came into the room when my dad and I were talking and I freaked out on her. She ruined my entire life! Because of her, I ended up here!" I shouted.

"Explain. How is it her fault? I don't disagree with you, but explain why you think this." He was speaking calmly, which pissed me off but was also keeping me semi-sane.

"She left a man who would have been a role model to me. But instead I get stuck with a bunch of men coming and going, and none of them ever treated me like a daughter. My mom didn't teach me self-love, and respect. I had no respect for myself when I met Darren. If I did, nothing would have happened between us. I wouldn't be anorexic. I wouldn't hate myself!" I let out a sob and covered my face to hide my tears; not that it was any use.

Dr. John waited until I stopped crying to speak. "Emily, I understand completely and agree to a certain extent that your mothers choice had a major impact on your life. She is still your mother, and she loves you. She didn't know this wouldn't be the right choice for you. She couldn't tell the future. I'm sure she doesn't want you here any more than you want to be here. At the time, she did what she thought was best. She made a mistake, a huge mistake with severe consequences, but a mistake nonetheless. So take time to forgive her. You can't keep her out of your life forever." His voice was soft, and he remained calm the whole time.

I took time to absorb what he said before I spoke. "You're right. I know that if she knew this was how I was going to turn out, she wouldn't have made the decision she did back then. But it doesn't change the fact that I did turn out this way, because of a decision she made. I can't forgive her any time soon. It would be stupid."

He nodded once more. "Emily if at any time you need to come and see me when we don't have an appointment, call my cell and we can arrange to meet as soon as possible okay? This is a big shock for you, so I understand why you're so upset." He handed me another tissue. "Unfortunately our session is up, and I do have another client to see." He truly did sound sorry that I couldn't stay longer.

"Thank you. Really, thank you." I said as I looked down at the floor. I was always too embarrassed to look people in the eye when I was crying. I left his office with tears still flowing down my cheeks.

Gemma and I spent the night sitting in the green room, curled up on a sofa with blankets and pillow, playing cards and talking about my parents. She let me cry on her shoulder until I couldn't cry anymore; Gemma was great like that. I didn't want to talk to anyone else, not even Caleb. He understood though, he always understood.

The rest of the week past uneventfully and it was Saturday once again. I was eager to go to art class because I had a lot of frustration to paint. I rushed out of my room to get to art as soon as I could.

Anna walked in a few minutes after I had arrived and she got her materials before sitting down right next to me. My body froze for a second; Anna had never sat this close to me before.

"I heard about what happened on Sunday." Her voice was so soft I wasn't sure if she had even spoken. She was dipping her brush in a cup of a water.

I nodded before I realized she can't hear me nod. "Yeah, it was an interesting day." Was about all I could muster. I was in shock that Anna was talking to me.

"I understand how you feel." She said this very hesitantly, as if she wasn't sure she wanted to continue with this conversation.

"You do?" I asked, bewildered. Was Anna about to tell me why she was here?

"Oh yes. You see, my mother took me away from my dad when I was very young, months old I believe. She was mentally ill though; she wasn't fit to have sole custody of me. My mom constantly moved us around, making it hard for my dad to keep up with where we were. She abused me for all of my childhood, until I was about seventeen. I could barely talk without getting a beating. She even threw me against a wall once, nearly gave me a concussion. Then my dad found me, and I lived peacefully with him for two years, until he died of a stroke. My mom took me back for a couple of months, until I found this place. I've been here ever since." She finished with a sigh.

I stared at her with my mouth slightly open. So this is why Anna was so quiet. The poor girl was afraid she was going to get smacked if she talked. I wanted to hug her and protect her from anything bad ever happening to her again.

"Thank you for telling me that Anna. You didn't have to do that." I mumbled.

"No, I think I did. You were feeling very alone, like no one knew what you were going through. Even in a mental hospital, you can feel alone."

Chapter 8

I was in my fourth month of treatment now, and I can honestly say I was doing a lot better. My dad had been coming to visit every Sunday since the day he first showed up. He told me about his search to find me; all the cities he went to. He told me about the endless nights he spent in dingy hotel rooms.

Anna and I had become closer ever since that day in art class when she told me her story. She even talked more in group and at meals. She was warming up to everyone now I think. She was quite an extraordinary person too. She had such big dreams; to travel, to write. There was never a boring conversation with Anna. I was becoming quite fond of her and decided that if I got out before her, I would most definitely come and visit her from time to time.

It was Monday morning and Gemma and I were getting dressed, almost ready for breakfast. I was observing myself in the mirror. Noticing how my clothes didn't hang off of me anymore. I didn't look like a rag doll. It felt kind of nice. My eyes weren't so sunken in to my head; my cheeks were fuller and had some color to them. My arms and legs no longer looked like straws.

"Hey Gemma?" I called from my side of the room; she was digging in her closet for her other shoe.

"Yeah?" her voice sounded muffled.

"I'm not fat...am I?" I didn't really mean this as a question; more of reassurance.

Gemma immediately straightened up and stared at me. It was as if she was seeing me for the first time. "No, Emily." She said softly. "You are most certainly not fat."

I nodded, tugging at my shirt. "I didn't think so either."

Seconds later, I felt Gemma's arms wrap around my neck. "I'm so glad you finally realized this!" she exclaimed as she released me from her grasp. There were tears in her eyes.

"Me too." I smiled and hugged her once more.

"Hey Gem, your scars are starting to fade." I pointed out. It was true; there weren't so many little white lines on her arms anymore and the pink ones were starting to turn white.

She smiled. "Yeah, you know before I was in here, I used to get so upset if my scars started to fade, but now, I'm glad that they are. It's erasing a past that I don't want to remember."

We walked down to the cafeteria for breakfast, and I grabbed a plate of French toast (two pieces), some scrambled eggs and two pieces of bacon. Gemma and I joined the rest of the girls at our usual table. Isabel had been much nicer to everyone since that day her and I talked months ago. She was even starting to become a friend. Before I started eating, Gemma announced that I didn't think I was fat. All of the girls clapped and patted me on the back; telling me again and again that I am nowhere near fat.

I looked down at my plate, and made my decision. I started with my scrambled eggs, they would be easy to finish. I took a break in between eating my scrambled eggs and my French toast, to see if I really wanted to go through with this. After realizing I felt okay with the eggs in my stomach, I continued to cut off a piece of my French toast. It was hot, and somewhat gooey inside my mouth. I closed my eyes, as if this would savor the taste. I realized how much I love French toast. I took another bite, after another. Before I knew it, my French toast was gone; both pieces. Again, I paused, and decided I felt okay with the eggs and now French toast in my stomach. I picked up a piece of bacon and ripped it in half. It wasn't too crunchy, and was easy to swallow. I repeated this procedure with the second piece as well. After taking the last bite of bacon, the realization of what just happened dawned on me. *I ate my first full meal in about eight months.*

The entire table was staring at me, and soon broke out into applause. Gemma was practically in tears of joy, and even Isabel was smiling at me. Leila looked proud and jealous at the same time. Anna gave me a nod of encouragement. This really happened. I ate a full meal. *Wow.*

I felt someone tap me on the shoulder, and when I turned around, it was Caleb's radiant smile that greeted me.

"I heard someone ate their first full meal?" he asked, pulling me in for a hug and giving me no time to answer. I could smell a trace of cigarettes and cologne on his shirt. I breathed in heavily, never wanting to forget this scent. I realized that being in Caleb's arms felt like home.

"Yeah. I guess I did." I breathed as he released me from his grasp.

"Emily, I am so incredibly proud of you!" his smile never fading.

I felt euphoric, triumphant and strong for the first time in a long time and I didn't want this feeling to go away. "I'm proud of me too." I truly meant it.

My meeting with Dr. John came quicker than I expected and I practically ran to his office. I couldn't wait to tell him what happened at breakfast today. Caleb and Gemma said we were going to celebrate tonight, and I was excited to see what they had planned. Nothing could ruin today. I wouldn't let anything ruin today!

I opened the door to his office, practically out of breath. "Dr. John!" I breathed, as I sat down on the couch.

"Emily? Are you alright?" he looked at me with concern etched on his face.

"I am fantastic! Do you want to know why?!" I was practically shrieking with happiness.

"Always." He replied.

"I ate my first full meal today! My first full meal in months! Isn't that great?!" I exclaimed.

"That is superb! I am so glad to hear this and I am so very proud of you!" Dr. John wiped a tear from his eye as he spoke. "This really is a big achievement for you Emily. You've been recovering so quickly; it's wonderful."

The rest of my session we just talked about my dad and how our visits were going. I also told Dr. John that I noticed I didn't look fat today. He said I'm making a great and quick recovery. I had the rest of the day to myself and I wanted to be away from everyone so I could really take in what happened this morning.

Gemma was at her therapy session when I got back, so I had my room to myself. Our room had been filled with our artwork over the month, and clothes were all over the floor. The sun was shining through our window, giving the room a natural glow. I flopped down on my unmade bed and stared at the white ceiling.

ate my first full meal. Did this mean that I would have to start doing this every day? I don't know if I was quite ready for that yet. Maybe I would go day by day. Or meal by

meal. Yes, that seems reasonable. I'll see how I feel before every meal, and decide if I can eat a full meal again. I can handle that.

I still couldn't believe I ate my first full meal. I hadn't eaten a full meal in months, and I actually kind of missed it. I didn't feel weak anymore. I felt happy not being in constant state of hunger. I couldn't feel the food sitting in my stomach, or the calories running to different parts of my body. I didn't want to be that sick again, I was starting to like being healthy. Well, sort of healthy.

Caleb seemed so happy for me today. The thought of his name brought a smile to my pale lips. Caleb. I knew for a while now that I liked him. I care about him. But it still bugged me that he knew why I was here and I didn't know why he was here. It was unfair. We've been through quite a bit in the four months I've been here, and we've formed a close bond. I feel like I have a right to know. Maybe I'll ask him if he can tell me, since I made such a big accomplishment today. It was worth a shot.

"Hey. So we decided to celebrate before dinner, so let's get our booties down to the rec room!" Gemma said as she walked into our room.

"Okay." I got up off my bed and put my shoes on.

All of our friends were there and everyone was grabbing me and hugging me, giving me congratulatory high fives. I just wanted to find Caleb.

"Emily." Alex's voice called from behind me.

"Hey!" I gave him a brief hug. I hadn't really talked to him lately.

"I'm proud of you. Ya know, for eating a full meal today." He said shyly, a blush creeping up his neck.

"Thank you, Alex." I smiled sweetly and gave him another hug.

We played an intense round of Twister, and then had an unofficial group meeting where we talked about everyone's progress. We all migrated to the green room to watch the start of the sun set and just chat. It was really relaxed, and it was a chance to see the relationships everyone had formed. We were a family now more than ever. I felt a knot form in my chest, and I started tearing up. I'm going to miss everyone when I eventually leave. They've all been so supportive of me throughout my time here, and I wouldn't see them every day, like this, once I left. Of course we would keep in contact, but it wouldn't be the same.

I shook the thoughts out of my head, remembering this was not supposed to be a bad day. The party didn't last much longer, as it was time to go to dinner. We all filed out in our little groups to go to the cafeteria. Gemma and Caleb joined either side of me and I smiled at them both, thinking I had lucky I was to have such fantastic friends.

I ate most of dinner (beef stew with a biscuit), but there was still some of my stew left. Nobody was disappointed though, and neither was I. Apparently, one full meal was good enough for today.

After dinner, I told Gemma I wanted to spend some time with Caleb. She said it was fine, she had a headache anyway and wanted to go lay down. I thanked her and caught up with Caleb walking down the hall way.

"Caleb!" I shouted, causing him to turn around.

"Hey!" He always looked happy to see me.

"Want to hang out for a little bit?" I was trying to sound casual so he didn't think anything was abnormal.

"Yeah, sure. Want to go to the green room?" he suggested, pointing to the doorway of the rec room.

"Nah. I'm kind of done being around people. Can we go to the quieter rec room down the other hallway?" It was a bit of a white lie, and far-fetched, so I hoped he would buy it.

He looked confused for a moment, but agreed all the same. We walked the opposite way of the noisy rec room with just silence between us. I could feel my heart rate speeding up. I was already becoming nervous about asking him. Shit. Could I actually do this? I was having such a good day. But at the same time, I really wanted to know. It had been bugging me for weeks now, and I couldn't contain it any longer. Yes, I had to ask. I just had to be straight forward and ask him. I could do this, I tried to tell myself but I knew it was a lie. My palms were sweating, and I wiped them on my jeans, hoping he wouldn't notice.

Caleb opened the door of the rec room and let me go in first. It was dimly lit, as no one ever used it. The set up was the same except there was no T.V. I sat down on one of the couches and placed a pillow on my lap.

"You're nervous about something." Caleb smirked as he sat down next to me.

"Huh? No I'm not." I tried to say without blushing again, but I knew I failed.

"Yes you are. Whenever you're nervous, you put a pillow on your lap if you have one. I've seen you do it at least once a week in the rec room." He knew he was right as the a smile played across his lips.

"Okay, fine, I'm nervous." I better start being honest now.

"Well, what are you nervous about?" he asked.

I sighed and looked away from him. "Okay, so I was thinking…about you today. And-"

"Wait, you were thinking about me?" he interjected.

"Yes." I snapped. "Anyway, I was thinking about how it's unfair that you know why I'm here and get to witness my recovery, but I don't know why you're here and I don't know what you're recovering from." I spoke the last part very fast, so fast I had hoped he didn't understand me.

He frowned and scratched his chin. I think he was considering whether he was going to tell me or not. I held my breath the entire time he did this. Sweat beads were forming on my forehead, and my heart was going to pound out of my chest any minute.

"You're right." He said, looking me right in the eye.

"I know it's a lot to ask and you've told me time and time again that you don't want to but I really think- wait, did you say yes?" I asked, realizing I hadn't even really heard him.

He nodded, stifling a laugh.

"Oh. Sorry. I wasn't really paying attention…" I whispered.

"I could tell." He giggled. His laugh was so cute.

"So…why are you here?" I asked awkwardly.

He took a deep breath and began his story.

"Everything started with my dad's death when I was eleven. My sister was nine, so she didn't fully understand what had happened, but she understood my dad wasn't coming back. My mom, lost it and went into a severe depression. It was bad; she stopped cooking and cleaning, even going to work. She only went often enough so that she wouldn't get fired. I had to take care of Karee, my sister. I became the man of the house. My mom stayed in bed a lot, so we never really saw her. Since she was hardly working, she wasn't bringing in much money, and we weren't able to receive life insurance checks right away I knew some friends who had tried getting me into drugs in the past, and I had always said no. But I knew that we needed the money, and I couldn't work. So, I went to my friends one day and told them I wanted in. I became one of the main drug dealers in my town, and I never told my mom about it. She didn't even notice the bills were being paid. Eventually, that stopped being enough, so I had to find another way to bring in money. I was fifteen and friends with this one senior. He knew about my situation and said he could help me out. He took me to a male strip club that he worked at and got me a job under the table. I made tons of tips, and it was enough combined with the drugs to get us by. I sold and stripped for about a year, until I got busted. Luckily, my lawyer got me the deal of going to therapy instead of juvie. I started out with out-patient and only went a

couple times a week. But then I got caught selling again about six or eight months later, so they put me into here. I was really resistant to treatment at first, but I came around after about a year."

I didn't know what to say when he finished speaking, so I just sat there and stared at him for a second.

"I didn't really want to tell you because I was afraid you'd see me differently afterwards, and I was right…" he said sadly.

"No. No, I don't see you differently. I just wasn't expecting that. I didn't know what to expect actually. But I think it was very admirable of you to take of your family. You had to do what you had to do, even if it landed you here. What about your mom and sister now?"

"They're both in separate mental hospitals. Karee got taken away by the state after I was put into in-patient, and my mom was put into a mental hospital. Karee later went to a mental hospital. She had developed a lot of issues from living alone with my mom." I could tell how painful it was for him to talk about it.

"We don't have to talk about this anymore. I don't want to ruin your day. Thank you…for trusting me enough tell me Caleb. It really means a lot to me…" I reached out and touched his arm. He looked up at my touch and smiled briefly.

"You're easy to trust. Plus you had a fair point. I knew along why you were here recovering, and you had no idea what I was progressing from. It was only fair. I'm glad I did though. Not even all of group knows. It's just you and my therapist now." He chuckled, trying to show he wasn't affected by our conversation.

felt bad, I truly did. He probably had thought about all this in such a long time, and it brought back so many painful memories for him. I leaned and hugged him tight. I couldn't form the words to apologize, so I hoped he could feel how sorry I was. His arms wrapped around my back, and he squeezed me tight. We sat like that for what seemed a long time, and I felt like I was safe from every cruel thing in the world.

drew back a couple of inches, releasing myself from his hug, but his arms were still around me. Half of his face was lit, while the other was slightly shadowed. His pink lips were forming a slight frown, and his eyes were almost black right now; as they always were when he was upset. There were tiny scars of acne that hadn't made an appearance in years along his forehead and chin. We looked at each other; studied each other for a few seconds longer. I couldn't tell you who made the first move, but the distance was closed between us, and I finally felt his warm lips on mine. His kiss was soft, and gentle. I could hear him breathe a sigh of relief, as if he had been waiting a long time to do this. The butterflies in my stomach soared to new heights as Caleb's hands pressed into my back. Our lips broke apart, and we looked at each not shocked at all. Instead he smiled at me and pulled me in for another hug.

We had talked some more after the kiss, and thankfully everything between us still felt normal. We had to go back to our rooms, as it was going to be lights out soon. We held hands walking down the hallway, and didn't say a word. Silence with Caleb was comfortable; sometimes even welcoming.

"Goodnight." He said softly as we approached my room.

"Goodnight." I replied, turning to walk into my room.

Gemma was sitting up in her bed, watching me as I walked in, a smile on her face.

"Tell me, EVERYTHING!" she said.

I laughed. She was so cute when she got excited about this stuff.

"Well," I said, sitting down on my own bed, and grabbing my pajamas. "I can't tell you everything, because some of it is confidential information. But I can tell you that we kissed."

Gemma let out a squeal, and clapped her hands to her mouth.

"No you didn't!" she gasped.

"Oh, but we did."

She smiled, and looked as though she had been waiting for this to happen for a long time; which honestly, she probably had. I pulled my pajamas on and climbed into bed. I was actually exhausted, and couldn't wait to fall asleep. For once, my good day did not get spoiled. I would be going to sleep with a smile on my face tonight, and the trace of Caleb's lips tickling mine.

The rest of the week was uneventful. Caleb and I had to act normal, as they frowned upon PDA. I managed to eat all of my lunch on Thursday, but that was it. Though I was starting to slowly like how I looked. My dad came as usual on Sunday and I told him all that had happened in the past week. He was so proud of me and swore that when I got out, and if I felt up to it, he would take me out to dinner. Sometimes he brought me flowers or a cute stuffed animal for my room. I don't even think that he was trying to make up for lost time, because he knew that was impossible. You can't get time back. But he was here now, and if he was going to be in my life, he was going to be as involved as possible.

Tuesday was going as normal as it could go until Gemma disappeared after lunch. I don't know where she went, but we always hung out after lunch. I didn't mind much because I just hung out with Caleb instead. Gemma came back around three, and she seemed really distant.

"Gemma?" I asked cautiously. "Are you okay?"

"Huh? Yeah. I'm fine. Let's watch T.V. I think She's the Man is on today." She barely even looked at me when she spoke, that I couldn't believe her.

"Gem. Seriously, what's up?" she couldn't just lie to me; not right to my face.

"Let it go. It's nothing." She said mindlessly as she turned on the T.V.

Annoyed, I agreed to let it go and return to Caleb in the green room. She didn't want to tell me, fine. Though it wasn't fair seeing as I told her everything whenever something major happened. I knew it was her choice though. It was her life, and if she wanted something private, then that was her decision. I just thought being her best friend, she would tell me.

Later, at group, Gemma was still acting weird. She barely talked, and she snapped at me whenever I asked her why she was acting weird. I decided I wasn't taking it anymore. After group, I dragged her back to my room. We were going to talk about this whether she wanted to or not.

"Emily! I told you to let this go!" she yelled as I yanked open our door.

I slammed the door and turned to face her. "Gemma, I have told you everything about me. Anything major that's happened, you're the first person to know. Why can't you tell me this? I'm your best friend!" I sounded wounded, and honestly I was.

"Um if you remember correctly, you CHOSE to tell me all of that stuff. I never bugged it out of you like you've been doing to me all day! I let you come to me. There's a difference, Emily." She retorted, her hands now on her hips. Her face was growing red with rage.

"I wanted to tell you because you're my best friend!" I argued.

"And you're mine, Emily. I just didn't want to tell you right when you wanted to know." She spoke softer this time; hinting we weren't really fighting anymore.

"I'm sorry." I sighed. "I shouldn't have bugged you about it. It's just...I can't wait to tell you when something happens to me, good or bad, and I thought it was the same way for you."

"It is. It is. It's just...it's really big news and I hadn't even wrapped my head around it when you started badgering me. I need more time than you Em." She hugged me as she spoke.

"I'm sorry." I said again.

"It's okay."
"So...do you want to tell me your news?" I asked, hoping she would finally tell me.

She looked nervously around the room, and said so quietly I could barely hear her.

"I'm going home."

Chapter 9

"Wh-what?" I stammered. This couldn't be real. We only had a couple months together, and now she was leaving? She just couldn't.

"I'm going home…they told me today that I'm allowed." She repeated. I couldn't tell if she was excited or disappointed; I hoped the latter.

"Well…I don't want you to leave, but I am happy for you. You get to have a normal life again. Don't you?" I said, sitting down on my bed.

"Yeah, somewhat I guess. I have to live with my grandmother, until we go to court about my dad. Then depending how that goes depends if my life stays normal or not." She sounded worried, and I was worried for her too.

"I'm sure everything will be fine Gem. There's no way the court will let you live with your dad." I said reassuringly.

She bit her lip and looked away; I could tell she wasn't so sure. "I hope so…" her voice trailed off.

"Do you want to help me pack? And we can exchange numbers, for when you get out." She was trying to sound optimistic, but we both knew a part of her didn't want to leave.

Taking down her art work and taking off her bed sheets just felt so weird. Her clothes were packed in the suitcase, and her make-up was no longer on the dresser. After forty-five minutes of packing, Gemma's side of the room was bare. I tried not to think about it too much, as I hadn't even said good-bye to her yet. I had all night to mourn my half empty room.

We both gave the room one last look before walking to the front lobby. We didn't talk on the way there, both of us unsure of what to say. When we got to the lobby, there was an elderly woman in a purple shawl, waiting uncertainly by the reception window. Gemma and I turned to face each other. We exchanged pieces of paper with our phone numbers written on them.

"I'll call you when I get out." I smiled meekly, gripping the paper in my sweaty palm.

"Good. Work hard on getting better so I can see you soon." Her voice cracked while she spoke, though there were no signs of tears.

"I'm going to miss you…" I said softly.

Her green eyes found mine and I could see how painful this was for her.

"You're my best friend, Emily. Since day one. Don't ever forget that, okay?" her voice remained strong this time, and she pulled me in for one last hug.

I felt her arms wrap around me, I forgot how strong her grip was. Her hair spelled like lavender and mint; a scent I'll miss. I buried my head in her neck and tried not to cry. She squeezed me once more before letting me go. She sniffled and picked up her bag.

"I'll see you." She said, before turning to meet her grandmother.

"Bye Gem." Was all I could manage before I turned around to walk to our...*my* room.

I opened the door and already forgot Gemma's stuff wasn't there. It was still haunted with her presence though. No more dark purple sheets. No more clothes spewing out of the closet doors, or art work on the wall. No more magazines on her nightstand. It was all gone, and so was she.

I went over to my bed and got underneath the covers. I pulled them close to my chest and breathed in deeply. The tears came before I could stop them, and I didn't bother trying to. My chest grew tight, and I fought for air. My body shook, and my face grew hot. I don't think I had cried like this since I got here. I could feel my heart breaking and my mind growing fuzzy. I cried myself to sleep that night, with Gemma's green eyes and lavender scented hair filling my mind.

The next morning I woke up, expecting to see Gemma, but the pain in my chest reminded me that she wasn't there, nor would she be coming back. I didn't want to think about if I would be getting a new roommate, and I hoped that I wouldn't. I wasn't ready for that yet. I pulled on a pair of worn out jeans and a sweatshirt, then tied my hair in a messy bun. At least Gemma's leave would give me something to talk about with Dr. John today.

I walked to Caleb's room, implying that I wanted him to walk with me to breakfast. He didn't even have to ask; he was already dressed and ready to go. We didn't say anything on the way to the cafeteria, and I was thankful for his silence. I hadn't told him that Gemma left, but he could tell by the way I looked that I wasn't in the mood for talking.

The girls table was silent without Gemma's laughter, and I dreaded sitting there without her. I grabbed my breakfast, told Caleb I would meet with him after we were done eating and headed over to my table. Isabel was the first to speak to me.

"Hey...how are you?" she asked cautiously. At least she didn't make some snide comment.

"Fine I guess." I didn't really know how to answer that question, so I used my default answer.

None of the other girls dared saying anything, and again, I was grateful. It was nice that they were sympathetic, but I just didn't feel like talking about it right now. Gemma is my best friend, and we had become so close. It just felt weird without her here. We spent the rest of breakfast eating in silence; the only sound was the chewing of our food. One by one, we cleared the table, until finally it was only Isabel and I.

"So tell me the truth, how are you really doing?" Isabel asked, slurping the milk from her bowl.

I sighed. "I don't know. My best friend just left." I snapped.

Isabel stared at me, and I could tell she didn't take offense to my harsh words. "Well, I'll be here if you want to talk. You know where to find me." She said as she got up from the table.

I had barely touched my cereal and toast, and felt somewhat guilty. Gemma would kill me if she knew I wasn't eating on account of her absence. So I decided, for Gemma, to finish my breakfast.

Caleb and I decided to go to the other rec room; I didn't feel like being around people much. We just lay on the couch and cuddled. We spoke very few words; the silence between us had always been comfortable. He stroked my hair away from my face repeatedly, and I felt my body relax at his touch. My head was against his chest, with both my arms wrapped around his chest. If I could, I would lay here forever. I breathed in his scent, and closed my eyes. He was always so warm, and his arms were like barriers from the rest of the world. At least I still had him.

My appointment with Dr. John went as expected. We talked about how I was dealing with Gemma's absence.

"Am I going to get a new roommate?" I asked hesitantly, not entirely sure if I wanted to know the answer.

"It's in consideration." Dr. John said, frowning. "Why? Do you not want another roommate?"

I picked a piece of lint off the couch and flicked it onto the floor. "I don't know." I mumbled. "I'm still getting used to living alone."

"Well, I can try and make sure you don't get a roommate, but I don't have much power. So if you do get a new roommate, please treat her kindly and with respect. I know you're hurting, but it wouldn't her fault."

"I know. I wouldn't be mean to her." I said absent-mindedly. My mind was wandering back to Gemma again.

"Good." He replied.

Our session ended, and I made the long walk back to my room. I didn't feel like being around the girls, and Caleb wasn't around for me to hang out with; he had a progress report meeting.

I avoided looking at Gemma's side of the room, and plopped down on my bed. Burying my face in my pillow, I let out a sigh. I felt pathetic for being this sad, but at the same, I don't have the one person I went to for everything now. She had become my rock, she held me when I cried, listened as I rambled on. Sure Caleb was still here, and I was grateful that he's so wonderful to me, but it's just not the same.

After lying there, staring at the wall for half an hour, I decided this was not the way I should be dealing with this. Gemma taught me to be strong, and this was certainly not being strong. I would see her again, once I got out. I just had to focus on getting better; and that's exactly what I would do.

I spent the rest of the day playing pool with Caleb and the guys. They were such a good distraction, and everyone was glad to see me amongst the living. Alex even joined in for a couple of days; something he had never done before. Caleb stood right next to me, kissing the top of my head. We all yelled in victory when Alex won. I'll never forget the grin on Alex's face.

Anna and Leila were in the green room, sitting by a window, chatting. They were sitting quite closely; whatever they were talking about seemed to be important. I decided to leave them alone. Isabel however, was nowhere to be found. I found this strange, as she was always in the rec room, flirting with one guy…or two. I decided to go and look for her.

I checked the other rec room but she wasn't there, so I went to check the court yard. Sure enough, there she was. Curled up on a bench, with her head resting on her knees. I wondered if I should intrude; it looked like she wanted to be alone. I decided against it, and stepped into the court yard. It was chilly outside, and I wondered how she wasn't wearing a jacket.

"Isabel?" I called, walking towards her slowly.

I heard her sniffle before she turned to face me. Her face was red and blotchy, and I could tell she had been crying. "Oh. Hi." She used the back of her hand to wipe a tear.

"This is a stupid question, but, are you okay?" I regretted it as soon as the words came out of my mouth. Of course she wasn't okay.

She laughed. "Well, not really. No." At least she wasn't mad at me.

"Do you want to talk about? I know we do enough of that here already but…it's probably different talking to someone who doesn't take notes every time you speak."

Again, she laughed. "Sure, but you probably won't understand."

"Try me." I said.

She took a deep breath, as if preparing herself for what she was about to say. "I found out that my rapist was found not guilty, so he's not going to jail. He's not getting probation, nothing. He's completely free. Yet here I am, locked up in a mental hospital. I know life isn't fair but…this is just wrong." She said angrily.

My heart went out to her; I didn't know exactly how she felt, Darren was locked up. I thought of what to say, and wrapped one arm around her shoulders.

"Isabel, I can't explain to you why this happened. But the police, and your parents, and your therapist, will keep you safe. I wish I had more to say…" I said apologetically.

"Thanks Emily. You didn't have to come looking for me. You're a good person." She said softly.

We sat like that for a while; her head against my shoulder, my arm around hers. We didn't say anything; we just sat there; staring at the trees and birds building a new nest. The flowers were bending in the soft breeze and the sun was beginning to set. Finally, I suggested we go back inside. She agreed, and we linked arms as we walked through the doors. I think we both felt a little better; now knowing we had someone else we could talk to.

I asked Isabel if she wanted to go to the rec room, but she said no. She walked back towards her room, and I went back to Caleb and the rec room. I think he would be happy to hear about Isabel and me.

When I walked into the rec room, Caleb was standing by the pool table, his eyes fixed on Alex, who was about to make his next move. Alex had his eyes focused on the eight ball, and his tongue was sticking out. I laughed before walking over to Caleb.

"So, I just talked to Isabel." I said with a smile.

He looked shocked. "Really?!"

"Yeah, she was having a rough day so we talked for a bit." I said, leaning back against the wall.

"I'm really glad you two aren't at each other's throats anymore." He said.

I rolled my eyes. "We haven't been mean to each other for months. We were just…not particularly close before today."

He gently nudged me in the ribs. "I'm just teasing you. But it really is cool of you to reach out to her like that."

We spent the rest of the night cheering Alex on in pool; who was easily becoming one of the best players at Reach for the Stars.

The rest of the week went by as smoothly as it could possibly go. Isabel and I had begun to hang out a bit more, and I was back to eating at least one full meal a day. I still thought about Gem every day, and I missed her just as much as the day she left. I didn't cry when looking at her side of the room, and I didn't expect her to walk through the door anymore.

After art class on Saturday, I was walking back to my room, when I noticed the door was open. Strange, I thought I closed it before I left. I always closed my door when I left my room. Maybe Caleb or someone had come looking for me. As I grew closer, I heard a girl's voice coming from inside my room. She was…humming to herself? What the hell is going on?! When I reached my door way, the realization of what was happening hit me. Boxes were scattered around Gem's side of the room. The girl had her back to me, and continued humming; she didn't even know I was there. Clothes were hung in the closet, and a poster or two was already taped to the wall. The girl was frail, like how I used to be. Her elbows and knees were knobbly, and her legs and arms were like sticks. What was left of her hair appeared to be a valiant shade of auburn, and her skin was practically white as snow. I took in the figure of the girl standing across from me; I guess have a new roommate.

"Erm, hi…" I said awkwardly, still standing in my door way.

The girl jumped, and spun around quickly. "Oh gosh, hi! Are you Emily? My roommate?" her voice was loud, and strong. It was quite unexpected from such a small body.

"Yes. I'm assuming you're my new roommate?" I waved my arm at the scattered boxes.

She blushed. "Yes. I'm Marilanne. You can call me Mari for short."

Well, Marilanne, it's nice to meet you." I was careful to shake her hand, not wanting to break any bones.

She gave me a strained smile before returning to her boxes. I considered not helping her, leaving her to her own devices, but then I recalled my first day here. Gemma was so friendly, and welcomed me with open arms. She helped me unpack my very few things. It wasn't Marilanne's fault that Gemma left, no need to treat her like it was.

"Do you want some help?" I asked kindly. Crossing to that side of the room for the first time since Gemma left.

"Sure." She blushed again. She pushed a box my way, and told me to just hang all of her clothes in the closet. I did as I was told.

I tried to figure out Marilanne, as I was putting away her clothes. Did she know she needed to be here? Or was she still in denial, like I was? I couldn't just ask her, that'd just be awkward. I decided to see how she acted; but from the sound of things right now, she knew her place, which was here.

It only took us another twenty minutes to finish unpacking her things, and I was facing a side that was completely different from Gemma's. Everything was pink; her bed sheets, her curtains, pillow cases, everything. There was nothing wrong with it, it just wasn't what I had been used to seeing for four months.

"Now that we're done unpacking, I could show you around?" I suggested.

"Okay." Her voice was suddenly small and timid.

I led her down to the rec room and green room; I wasn't brave enough to announce her arrival like Gemma had done. Then we went to the cafeteria, followed by the courtyard and the second rec room. I showed her the Star Board in the lobby, and her eyes were wide with fear. I couldn't blame her, I remember how overwhelming this all was to me.

"Can we go back to the room now?" she asked; sounding much like a frightened child.

I nodded and led her back to our room. I told her I was going down to the rec room, but I would be back soon. She was already curled up in her bed, shaking with sobs.

I felt bad for her, I really did. She didn't know anyone, probably didn't want to be here, and had new information shoved down her throat in a matter of hours. It was enough to make any mentally ill person cry.

Caleb approached me as soon as I walked into the rec room, enclosing me in his arms. You would think it's been years since I last saw him!

"So I have a new roommate." I said, wasting no time to bring up the subject.

"I'm not surprised. They usually fill up any sort of empty room pretty quickly. How is she?" he asked.

I shrugged. "She was crying on her bed when I left. I'd comfort her, but it wouldn't really do much good. She needs time to soak everything in."

He nodded in agreement. He didn't ask any other questions about her, and I knew he wasn't really interested. We decided to join some other kids in watching some weird sci-fi movie for the rest of the night. At nine o'clock, everyone dispersed back to their rooms, and I was half expecting to find Marilanne asleep. Surprisingly, she was awake, sitting upright on her bed, as though she had been waiting for me.

"Hi?" I said awkwardly.

"Are you like me?" she asked, her voice once again confident and unwavering. "You don't like to eat?"

I pondered her question for a moment. "I still don't like to eat, but I'm not afraid to anymore."

She nodded. "How long did it take you to start eating again?"

I laughed, and immediately regretted it. "Sorry, I forgot you don't know all the rules yet. I started eating the day I came here. Everyone has to, even ED girls. One of the major rules." I explained, watching her expression change to horror. It reminded me of me on my first day.

"I have to eat?" she asked softly.

"Yes. You don't have to eat the whole meal, but you do have to eat some of it." Her expression softened a bit.

"Oh. Okay." She blushed quite easily I noticed.

"Look, Marilanne, I know that food seems scary right now. You get that uneasy feeling in your stomach when food is just sitting in there. You think you can feel the calories travel all over your body. You feel disgusting, and no matter how many meals you skip, you never get any skinnier. But take a look at me, I've been eating full meals for about a week or so, not too long, and I'm starting to realize that I don't blow up like a balloon afterwards. Look at me and tell me if you think I'm fat." I insisted.

She stared at me for a second or two. "You're not fat all."

"Exactly. I used to be in the same boat as you. I don't expect you to recover tonight, or tomorrow or even next week. But at least try to get better while you're here okay? You're here for a reason. Promise me, you'll work towards getting better."

"I promise."

About three weeks later, I was called down to Dr. John's office. I found it odd because it was a Tuesday, and I don't see him on Tuesdays. I suspected it might be a progress report.

Over the past few weeks, I had been eating one full meal a day, and at least one third of my other two meals. I got into the habit of taking walks around the building and outside. Not because I thought I would get fat from eating, but to help Marilanne. She wanted to take walks so she didn't feel like the food was just sitting in her; exactly like I did in the hospital.

I walked in to his office, and sat down on my usual spot. He had papers spread out all over his desk, and he was rubbing his temples.

"Dr. John?"

He looked up, slightly startled. "Oh, Emily, hi. I'm sorry, I was just filling out some paper work. Why are you here?"

"You called me down here, remember?" I said, utterly confused.

He paused for a moment, trying to remember why I was down here. "Oh! Yes! Now I remember! I have some exciting news for you!" his mood was suddenly elated, and he practically jumped out of his seat.

"Okay, tell me."

A wide grin grew on his wrinkled face. "You get to go home today."

Wait, what? I hadn't even been here for six months, how could I be going home already? "Are you sure?" I asked, somewhat breathless.

"Absolutely sure. Your progress is astounding, and I got confirmation this morning."

I nodded, lost in my thoughts. Marilanne just came, and we were getting along so well. Then there was Caleb; he showed no signs of getting out soon, what would happen with us? I felt nauseous, and my head felt light as a feather. I didn't want to go home yet.

"You might want to start packing your things, your dad will be here soon." Dr. John's voice sounded miles away.

I felt like I was separated from my body; like I was watching myself walk back to my room to pack my things. *At least you get to see Gemma,* a voice said in my head. I stopped in the middle of the hallway. That's right; now that I was going home, I'd be able to see Gemma! My spirits brightened a bit as I continued the walk back to my room. I had no idea how I would tell Marilanne; I felt like she looked up to me, like a big sister almost. I would come and visit her though.

Thankfully, Marilanne wasn't in our room when I got back, so I had time to think about how I would say good-bye. Though it wouldn't be difficult for her to figure out when she would be greeted by half of our room being bare.

I was close to packing up my things when I heard light footsteps approaching the door way. A knot formed in my stomach, and tightness sprouted in my chest. I had to do this, but I didn't want to.

"What's going on? Where are you going?" Marilanne's voice sounded panicky.

I turned to face the small girl. "I'm going home. I got the news today, about an hour ago actually." I said, trying to sound nonchalant.

"You're leaving already?" she replied.

I nodded slowly. "I didn't expect it either, but yeah, I'm going home..."

"Well...lucky you then, huh?" she laughed uncertainly, sitting on the edge of her bed.

"Marilanne, I'm sorry I'm leaving you so soon. I don't want to...I like you. I like our daily walks, and helping you recover." I said earnestly.

She smiled. "I like you too Emily. You're a good person, you know that?"

I smiled back. "So I've been told. But listen, just because I'm leaving doesn't mean you can give up, okay?" I pointed a finger at her in a motherly fashion.

"I won't, don't worry. I'll keep going, just for you."

I looked at her sadly. "Do it for you too."

She helped me pack up the rest of my things, and carry them out to the lobby. I hugged her good-bye once more and I told her I would come and visit as soon as I could. I made her promise me once more to keep working on recovery. She insisted she would, and just like that, I left. My dad carrying my suitcase and a box, and me with the rest of my stuff. I realized something different about the two good-byes I had experienced in the past month; I said everything to Marilanne that Gemma couldn't say to me.

Caleb and I had already said our good-bye, as he had his appointment. I promised I would visit, and I gave him my number so he could call me as soon as he got out. We hugged for what seemed like forever, and even then, it didn't seem long enough. We never had enough time together.

"Are you excited to be going home?" My dad asked. There was no need for him to say he was excited; it was written all over his face.

"Sort of. I'm going to miss the friends I made." I said as walked to the car. The wind was blowing my hair in my face, and was biting against my cheeks. It was cold for an April afternoon.

"Well, you can keep in touch, I'll bring you down to visit." He smiled at me while loading my luggage in the trunk.

My dad was so wonderful. Apparently, he had already gone to my mom's house to collect all of my things, and had my room set up at his place. I was excited to live with him. I had no memories of him, and now was our chance to make some. I had a feeling he wouldn't be the nagging type; life with him could be really cool.

We began driving and I switched on the radio to my favorite station. We didn't talk much on the drive back, and I was fine with that. I had just seen him two days ago, so we had nothing to talk about. I watched the trees blur together as we sped down the highway. I couldn't stop thinking about Caleb and Marilanne, and my heart began to ache. I hoped that Marilanne stayed true to her promise. I reminded myself that when the time was right, I would be able to see Caleb on a regular basis. *I can't see him every day **now** though,* said the same annoying voice in my head. I frowned, annoyed with my conscious. I gave up on staying awake, as I would only think about Caleb and Marilanne; so I decided to try and get some sleep for the remainder of the car ride. I rested my head against the window, and shut out the world around me.

"Emily."

"Emily."

I felt a hand touch my shoulder lightly and I jumped, banging my head against something hard. "Huh?" I said groggily.

"We're home." The voice said.

I opened my eyes slowly, recalling that I had fallen asleep in the car. How long had I been sleeping? An hour? Two? The sun was starting to set, and I was shivering slightly. I unbuckled, and stretched. My dad was already unpacking my luggage from the trunk; the driver door still wide open. We were in a parking garage of what I could assume was his apartment building.

"Do you need help Dad?" I called from the passenger seat.

"Just grab your little bags, honey. I have the rest. If you could close the trunk though, that would be great." He said cheerfully.

My heart swelled as I realized how happy my dad was that he wouldn't be alone anymore. He had his daughter back in his life; something he had been hoping for for sixteen years.

I got out of the passenger seat, slamming the door behind me. I retrieved the rest of my bags and closed the trunk. My dad and I walked up the four flights of stairs to his floor,

and walked down what seemed to be an abnormally long hallway. We finally stopped in front of a room labeled 437, and dad unlocked the door. I didn't really know what to expect. A shabby, messy apartment that smelled like moth balls and sweat? Or a clean, organized apartment with no foul odors at all?

Luckily it was closer to the latter. The floors were wooden, and the walls were a maroon color. Pictures of me were hung all over the walls; I'd have to ask him about that. Curtains were hung over every window, and they were wide open, letting the evening sun shine in, giving the place a warm glow. The living room had white carpet, different from the rest of the apartment. A big flat screen sat in a corner, and two couches forming a V faced it. Magazines were scattered on the coffee table, and dirty dishes sat in the sink but that didn't matter. The place smelled like roses, and popcorn. I smiled; I could definitely call this place home.

Dad led me to my new room, which thankfully was right next to the bathroom. I opened the door and let out a small gasp. The walls were a royal purple, and the carpet matched the living room. A black chandelier hung from the ceiling, and black curtains hung over my window. Dark wood furniture was placed strategically around my room. This was beautiful. I laid my luggage on my bed, which was covered in purple sheets. I looked around once more, drinking everything in. I remembered to thank my dad.

"Hey Em, I'll order pizza, and pick out a movie, while you unpack, sound good?" my dad asked, as he popped his head into my doorway.

I sat up. "Sure, sounds great! I'm not picky!"

He smiled and disappeared to the living room. I sighed and stood up. The urge to call Gemma and tell her I was home was strong, but I resisted. It was my first night home, and my dad was so excited to spend real time with me. It could wait until tomorrow. Speaking of which, I need my cell phone. Leaving my suitcase opened on my bed, I went out to the kitchen.

"Hey dad," I said.

He held a finger up to me, and I saw that he was on the phone. "Twenty minutes? Great. Thank you." He clicked the end button, and put his phone on the counter. "What's up?"

"Well, I was just wondering if you have my cell phone. I need it to call Gemma tomorrow to tell her I'm home." I said.

"Oh yeah! Hold on a second." He headed to his bedroom, and I heard him fumble around in a drawer. A minute later he reappeared. "Here you go!" he said as he handed my phone to me.

"Thanks dad. I'm going to finish unpacking, just let me know when the pizza's here." I gave him a quick hug and walked back to my room.

I managed to unpack most of my belongings when my dad called that the pizza was here. I debated bringing my phone with me, but decided against it. I could check it in the morning.

My dad chose 'Up', one of my favorite movies. We sat on the couch, with a blanket over our legs, eating pizza right out of the box. I ate a whole slice, and dad patted me on the back, congratulating me. I even took a couple bites of a second piece. We didn't really talk during the movie; dad had never seen Up before tonight. He cried, and so did I.

I helped him clean up the pizza, and even helped him do the dishes that were already in the sink.

"Thanks for hanging out with me tonight, Em. It meant a lot to me that you chose to be here with me, instead of with Gemma." He said sheepishly.

"Don't thank me. I've waiting to spend real quality time with you all my life. I wanted tonight just as much as you." I said with a smile.

My dad hugged me, and we both agreed to call it a night. Today had been a weird one, and I just wanted to get a good night's sleep. I told myself I would call Gemma in the morning to see if she could hang out. My phone lay silent on my dresser, so I didn't bother checking it before I climbed into bed and drifted off to dreamland.

The next morning I woke up to the sun shining right in my eyes. I squinted, as I sat up and pushed my hair off of my face. Stretching, I looked at my alarm clock. 11:30 am it read. I flopped back down on to my pillow, relishing how refreshed I felt. I hadn't good sleep like that in a long time.

The thought dawned on me that I was supposed to call Gemma today, and just as I was about to get up to call her, my stomach growled. *After breakfast.* I thought. Pulling my covers back, I sat up and slowly got out of bed. I opened my door and didn't hear anything from the living room or kitchen. Maybe dad was still sleeping. When I got to the kitchen, I saw a note hanging by a magnet on the fridge.

Em,

We were out of milk, and I figured you'd need some for breakfast. I'll be back in a bit. Hope you slept well.

Love,
Dad.

I laughed and crumpled the note. Thankfully he had plenty of cereal choices; I went with Captain Crunch. I got a bowl and spoon ready for when he got back. Deciding the TV was good entertainment while I waited, I wandered over to the living room and plopped down on the couch. The Fresh Prince of Bel-Air was on, and I couldn't resist.

Fifteen minutes later, my dad walked in the door, his arm full of groceries. I ran to help him, and shut the door.

"I realized," he huffed "That since there are two people living here now, I need more food; that's why I was gone so long."

"Dad I don't really eat much right now anyway, remember?" I asked, pouring cereal into my bowl.

He scowled. "I plan on changing that."

We put away the groceries, and he poured himself a bowl of cereal. I watched the next episode of Fresh Prince with him, then told him I was going to call Gemma. He offered to give me a ride if I needed it and I thanked him.

I picked my phone up off my dresser and unlocked it. *10 missed calls. 8 text messages.* Weird. Everyone knew my phone was off for the past couple of months. I opened my missed call log and saw that the number wasn't programmed into my phone. It took me a second or two, but I realized the number was Gemma's. She obviously didn't know when I was getting out so she must have kept trying to reach me the past couple of weeks.

I opened the text messages, excited to see a sign of contact from Gemma. But the moment I read the first one, my excitement changed to horror. This couldn't be. *No, no, no.*

Emily? Are you out yet? God I hope you get out soon. I shouldn't have gone home yet. I wasn't ready. I can't do this.

I want to cut again. I'm trying not to, but it's hard. I hope you get out soon.

They just got worse from there. I prayed that she was okay. Tears were streaming down my face, as I pressed the call button. It rang three or four times before someone picked up.

"Gemma?!" I sniffled.

"No, this is her grandmother. Oh dear, is this Emily?" he voice sounded fragile.

"Yes." I replied. *Just let me talk to Gemma dammit.* "Is Gemma there? Can I talk to her? I need to know if she's okay." I was practically pleading with a woman I didn't know.

"I don't know how to say this sweetheart but…you can't talk to Gemma. She-"

"What do you mean I can't talk to Gemma?!" I asked angrily.

"You can't talk to her because she's not here anymore. She's gone." Her voice was flat.

"Gone? What do you mean gone? Gone where? With her dad?" I asked, extremely annoyed now.

"She…she was living with her dad, and she didn't want to be there anymore when he started beating her again. I tried to get her out, but her father is an intimidating man. I didn't even want her to live with him again. I got a call last night saying her father found her on the bathroom floor. She uhm, she committed suicide. She's gone…" her voice cracked as she spoke, and I could tell it was difficult for her to get the words out.

I stopped breathing, and my vision went blurry. More tears were silently racing down my cheeks and I didn't bother to stop them. There was a slight buzzing sound in my ears, and my stomach seemed to have disappeared. This couldn't be right. She couldn't be gone. She couldn't….she just couldn't!

I hung up the phone and walked mindlessly over to my bed. I curled up under my blankets, and let the sobs take over. I cried harder than I ever did at Reach for the Stars. My throat hurt from wailing, my snot was forming a pool on my top lip, my tears were soaking my pillow, and my body wouldn't stop shaking. I could hear my heart beat in my ears, and I was beginning to hyperventilate. I laid like that for a long time; not caring about anything anymore.

I heard my dad come in my room, and lay down next to me on my bed. I turned over, into his arms, and continued to sob. He stroked my hair, and just held me as I stained his shirt with my despair. My eye lids felt heavy, and my breathing was slowly. The tears were still flowing as I fell asleep once more.

I'm going to wake up, and find out it was just a bad dream. A really, really bad dream. I told myself. Rubbing my eyes, I sat up to find a tray at the end of my bed. A peanut butter and jelly sandwich and a glass of apple juice sat on it, along with a note.

Hey sweetie,

Here's something to eat in case you get hungry. When you're ready to talk, I'll be in the living room. Take your time.

I wanted to smile, I really did, but I just couldn't. I'd feel too guilty. The sight of sandwich made my stomach churn. My throat however, was dry. I picked up the apple juice and chugged. Smacking my lips, I sat it back down on the tray. I really wanted to see my daddy right now, and that's exactly what I did.

He was laying on one of the couches, hand on his stomach, zoned into ESPN.

"Daddy." I said in a small, squeaky voice.

He looked over at me, and jumped at once. "Come here." He said as he opened his arms.

I ran into them, trying to hold back the tears this time. He kissed my forehead before pulling away from me. "Come sit down." He guided me to the couch.

Turning off the T.V., he focused his attention on me. "What's going on Em?" he asked softly.

I wiped away a tear, and gathered my composure before speaking. "I tried calling Gemma this morning and-" I couldn't finish my sentence because I started crying again.

My dad stroked my arm, and calmed me down. "Take your time. Take a deep breath." He looked so sad.

"When I called, her grandmother answered. She…she told me that Gemma's gone. She committed suicide last night." I choked out the last few words before letting my sobs consume me once again.

My dad said nothing as he pulled me into his arms again. I didn't blame him for being speechless; after all, I was the speechless one a few hours ago.

"She texted me last night begging me to call her and I didn't. If I had called her, she might be alive right now!" I wailed.

'No, honey, no. Don't put the blame on you. It's not your fault." He cooed.

My dad held me until I stopped crying. "I'm going to call her grandmother and find out details about the funeral, okay?" he asked, holding on to my shoulders.

nodded and laid down on the couch, grabbing a tissue. I heard him offer his condolences and update Gemma's grandmother on how I was doing. Five minutes or so later, he returned to the room. He ruffled his hand through his hair and sat down next to me on the couch.

"So the viewing is tomorrow at seven p.m, and the funeral is on Friday at eleven a.m." He said calmly.

"Okay." Was all I could manage to say.

was scared. I had never been to a funeral before, and I didn't know what to expect. Obviously people dressed in black, and lots of crying; but what else would happen, I had no idea. My dad said he would go with me, and I don't think he understood how grateful was.

The next day around five p.m I began to get dressed for the viewing. My dad took me shopping earlier in the day for a new black dress; as all my clothes didn't fit me properly anymore. I hadn't eaten much since yesterday, and dad wasn't pestering me about it. He

understood. I yanked the comb through my brown curly hair, and tried to make it look decent; an impossible task.

At six-thirty, my dad and I were out the door and in the car, on our way to the second worst night of my life so far. He patted my knee every few minutes, while I just stared straight ahead; oblivious to the world around me.

Fifteen minutes later, we pulled up to the funeral home, and I suddenly felt like I was going to have a heart attack. I wouldn't know anyone here, and they wouldn't know me. My dad joined his hand with mine, and I felt the strength in each finger. If only he could pass some of that strength to me. As we approached the building, the clumps of people came into view. Some were chatting casually; how they were doing so I have no clue. Others were clutching tissues to their chest and weeping on each other's shoulders. I looked at my dad uncertainly, and he gave me what was supposed to be a reassuring smile.

Standing alone by the door of the funeral home, was a very short, thin woman with gray, curly hair. Her lipstick looked like it had been done by a five year old, and her blue eyes were watery. My dad and I approached her slowly, hoping she was Gemma's grandmother. Judging by the picture of Gemma in her hands, I could say that she was.

"Hi…I'm Emily." I said nervously, sticking out my hand.

She looked down at it before grasping it. Her hand was bony, and clammy. "Such a terrible occasion to meet you dear. I'm Amelia." She said sadly.

My dad introduced himself, and offered his condolences once more.

"Yes, it's quite terrible." Amelia said as she looked down at the picture of Gemma.

I couldn't do this. I had to. I couldn't not say good-bye to Gemma. A man came to open the doors, signaling we were allowed to enter. My hands shook as they found my dad's, and we walked in together. Amelia told me I should sit up front, and I felt awkward in doing so. Looking at the lack of people sitting in the front row, I could tell Gemma didn't have much family attending. I felt my heart break into smaller pieces than I ever thought possible.

A man stood in front of us all, and explained how the viewing would operate. It was open casket, and I couldn't decide if it was a good or bad thing. My heart was pounding in my ears, and I couldn't stop shaking. This was so terrifying. Someone was nudging to me go to the casket. I shook my head, and saw the man standing over me, looking slightly annoyed.

I got up, and walked to the casket. My legs felt like Jell-O and the casket seemed hundreds of feet away. I managed to make it to the casket without falling, and had to hang out to the side of it to prevent me from falling to the ground.

Her black hair was combed away from her face, and shone brightly in the lights hanging over her. Her eyes were closed, and her hands were on her chest. I didn't dare look at her wrists because I knew what I would find. Her skin was ghostly white, and sparkling slightly. She looked like the wrong kind of peaceful. She wasn't supposed to be here. She was supposed to be alive, reuniting with me, laughing, having deep talks with me, just like old times. Fresh tears like out of eyes, and I stroked her face. "Gemma." I whispered.

I felt someone walk up behind me and I knew my time with her was through. "Good-bye." I said, as I walked away from my best friend.

The funeral was no easier than the viewing. It felt so wrong, watching them lower her into the Earth. Her grandmother hadn't stopped crying since I saw her yesterday, and quite honestly neither did I. Prayers were said, and roses were placed on top of her casket. We all stood around in a circle, our eyes following the descendent of the casket. The air was warm and moist, dark clouds hanging above.

The ceremony was over as quickly as it started, and everyone milled around to say hollow good-byes. Amelia gave me a hug, and told me I could stop by any time. I thanked her and told her we would be checking in on her.

"You know, when Gemma was living with me, she talked about you an awful lot. You meant a great deal to her." Amelia said, touching my arm lightly.

"She meant…means a lot to me too. She's my best friend." I said.

Amelia smiled sadly, and said "Please don't think you didn't change her. You did, it's just…you have to know her father to understand this. I'm not saying what she did was right, but I understand."

I nodded, unsure of what to say.

"You were the only best friend Gemma ever had. You were special to her. You affected her greatly." She said before walking towards her car.

I watched her go; the only woman who was any reminder of Gemma. My dad grabbed my hand again and we walked towards the car. I got in, and rested my head against the window. Rain drops were starting to fall, and I could hear the slight patter as they landed on the window. I heard the faint rumble of the engine as my dad started the car, and we pulled out of the cemetery.

You were the only best friend Gemma ever had. Amelia's voice repeated in my head. I squeezed my eyes shut, and prayed I wouldn't start crying again. I forced myself to get lost in the rain drops and the blur of the town passing by; anything but to think about Gemma.

People often say that occasionally you meet someone who gives your life a whole new light. For me, that person was Gemma.

When I first entered Reach for the Stars, I was stubborn and in denial. I didn't think I belonged there, I didn't want to be there. Gemma made me realize how sick I was. She showed me what a true friend really was; always comforting me, learning about my past, waking me from my nightmares. She always showed me the bright side of things, always found the silver-lining in situations. She was and always will be my best friend; the person who gave my light a new life.

I will get better for you, Gemma. I will. I'm not giving up.

Epilogue

"One, two, three. One, two, three." I shouted over the music blasting in the studio. A group of girls danced and twirled around the room in front of me, in time with the music. They were getting better and better every week. The music ended and class was over.

"Okay, see you guys next week." I said as they filed out of the room. I went to my office, gathered my belongings and headed home.

Thankfully, my apartment was only a couple blocks from the dance studio, so I could walk to work. I climbed the six flights of stairs, and opened my apartment door.

"Hey sweetie." He called from the living room, still focused on the T.V. His feet up on the coffee table.

I dropped my keys in the bowl by the door, and hung my coat on the back of a chair. "Hi Caleb." I walked into the living room, sat down next to him on the couch and planted a kiss on his cheek.

I pretended like I was interested in the sitcom he was watching, but gave up when they made a crude joke. I knew not to bother him while he was watching his show. Besides, I needed to get changed from dance class. I threw on my favorite pair of jeans, a sweater and threw my hair up in a bun; my curly brown hair still as difficult as ever. My cheeks were red from the cold winter wind, and my eyes shone brightly in the glow of the bedroom light.

"Hey honey, I'm going out in a couple minutes. I'll be back later." I yelled from the bathroom; pulling the scale out from underneath the sink.

I stepped on the scale, not scared anymore of what the number would be. After a second or two, the number *143* flashed on the digital screen. I nodded, stepping off the scale, and returned it to its usual spot.

Caleb walked in to the bathroom just as I was putting the scale away. He gave me a disapproving look.

"Em, you look great! Why are you weighing yourself?" he asked.

"Caleb, you know why. I shouldn't have to explain it to you after all these months." I rolled my eyes at him, turning off the bathroom light.

It took him a few seconds but he remembered. "It's just that you haven't done it for months. I wasn't sure…" his voice faded, as he gave me an apologetic look.

I laughed. "With a husband who reminds me every day how beautiful I am, I doubt I'll ever go back to that." I patted him on the back.

"It's cold outside today!" he called, as I walked back to the kitchen.

"I'm aware." I said as I put on my jacket. I wrapped my scarf around my neck, and pulled on my gloves.

"I don't like you walking there…" Caleb said, now standing in the kitchen.

"Then come with me."

He shook his head. "This is your thing." He insisted.

"I'll call you when I get there, like I do every time." I told him, grabbing my keys and heading out the door.

"Love you!" I heard him yell, as the door closed behind me.

"Love you too!" I yelled back.

I stepped out on the street, blinded by the mid-afternoon sun, and began my walk. My heels clacked against the pavement, and I unwillingly tuned in to snippets of people's conversations as they passed. Cars were zooming by; dangerous on these city streets. The wind whipped through my hair, and I drew my scarf around my mouth and ears. I bustled through the crowd, in the hopes of reaching my destination sooner. I was naïve to think this would happen.

I was too busy looking down, watching the countless pairs of feet around me, that I didn't have time to see a pair heading straight towards me. A few seconds later, we collided.

"Ouch!" I yelled, clasping my hand to my head. That would surely leave a bruise.

"Sorry!" a man's voice said.

I looked up, and immediately lost my breath. Right in front of me, was a pair of dark, blue eyes. *Darren.*

I realized who he was before he recognized me, and wasted no time getting away from him. I left him standing confused, in the middle of the crowd. I hoped he never figured out who had just run in to.

I forced myself to calm down, as I continued walking. I was too far ahead now for him to even have a chance of catching up with me. Car horns beeped, and people were yelling into their cell phones. I never really took notice to how loud the city was. I loved it though; absolutely loved it. The constant noises of the city were always a distraction from the noises inside my head.

I finally reached the road that started to lead out of the city. Thankful that was somewhat closer to my destination, I slowed my pace; enjoying the change in scenery. There were no longer buildings on either side of me, or cars lining the streets. Instead there were fields, the occasional house and one or two people walking their dog. I still had about twenty minutes or so until I was there.

Realizing how long this walk was, I remembered why I had stopped doing this every week. I felt guilty at first, but it hurt less now. I no longer cried, instead there was just a knot in my stomach. The sun slowly beginning to set, and I knew I would have to call Caleb to come pick me up. He didn't like me walking home in the dark, and I didn't blame him.

A golden retriever barked from down the street, and a little girl shrieked. My heart sunk, as I remembered the doctor's visit years ago. My reproduction system hadn't been working properly since before I was in the hospital, so our chances of having kids were slim to none. We hadn't been lucky so far. It was something I constantly felt guilty about because Caleb wanted kids more than anything in the world; though he insisted that I was enough for him. We talked about adoption more than once but couldn't afford it.

I hurried past the house with the little girl playing in the yard, not wanting to dwell on the matter any longer. Fifteen minutes now. I hated the winter. I hated putting on layers of clothes just to stay warm. But I hadn't been here in months, I had to go. It was yet another thing I would feel guilty about.

A man walking his golden retriever gave me a friendly wave as he passed, and I simply smiled. Maybe if Caleb and I moved into a house someday, we could get a dog! He would love that; the thought made me smile.

My phone rang, and Dr. John flashed across the caller ID. I smiled.

"Your timing is amazing!" I laughed into the receiver.

"Oh no, what happened this time?" his voice sounded muffled on the other end.

"You'll never guess who I ran into on the street." I said.

"You're right. I won't. So tell me."

"Darren."

There was silence for a moment.

"Dr. John? You still there?" I asked.

"You're lying." He said in disbelief.

"I wish I was. I wasn't watching where I was going and I bumped into him. He didn't recognize me before I took off." I explained.

"He's supposed to be in jail for three more years. I don't know how he got out early..." he sounded angry and puzzled.

"Well, he didn't recognize me so-"

"Emily, promise me that if you see him again, you'll call the cops." He urged.

"Okay?"

"I mean it. It's my job to make sure he never hurts you again. Call the cops if you see him again, understand?" his voice was stern.

"You know, I'm not eighteen years old anymore. You could start talking to me like the thirty year old woman that I am." I teased.

"Yeah well, you're still as stubborn as you were when you were eighteen." He teased back. Dr. John had become like a second father to me.

"Bye, Dr. John. Thanks for checking in." I said.

"Always." He replied before hanging up.

I shut my phone and shoved it back in my pocket. I was almost there. Shadows were cast from the trees and houses nearby and the branches swayed in the wind. Finally, I reached my destination. I pushed open the giant, heavy black gates, and pulled out my cell phone once more.

"Hey. I'm here. Can you pick me up though? It'll probably be dark by the time I start to walk home." I asked Caleb.

"Sure. I'll leave in say ten minutes?"

"Okay. I'll be here."

Hundreds of tombstones appeared before me, and I started up the path to the top of the hill. Squirrels scurried around the base of trees, gathering the last of the nuts. There was no wind in the graveyard; just complete stillness. Once up the hill, I followed the path to the right and downhill a bit.

I stopped at a grave three tombstones from the end of a row. I kneeled in front of it. Grass had fully grown in over the years, and there were fresh flowers placed in front of the tombstone; though they were beginning to wilt from the cold.

A carving of two angels was at the top of tomb, followed by:

Gemma Thompson
A True Angel
July 12th 1993- April 23rd 2012

I remember the day, twelve years ago, when I was here for her funeral. I still didn't like to think about it. I shut my eyes and took a deep breath. I hadn't been here in months, and it felt a little strange to be back. Clouds were creeping their way in, and I was afraid it was going to rain. I'd have to make this quick.

"Hi, Gem. I know I haven't been here in a while. It's a long walk, and stubborn me refuses have Caleb drive me. He doesn't want come anyway. He feels like he's intruding."

Silence.

"Dance classes are going well. I think the girls will be ready for their recital at the end of January."

Silence.

"Oh yeah! I bumped into Darren on the way here! Don't worry, he didn't recognize me. It scared me though."

Silence.

"I miss you. A lot. I always miss you. I've missed you every day for the past twelve years." I whisper.

Silence.

"Everyone from Reach for the Stars is doing really well. We still get together every month and go out to dinner, or see a movie. It's nice. I wish you were here to come with us though."

Silence.

'Anyway, I just thought I should tell you…I weigh 143 pounds now."

Silence.

smile to myself, and a ray of sunshine breaks through the clouds and I know, Gemma's
smiling too.

CPSIA information can be obtained
at www.ICGtesting.com
Printed in the USA
BVHW071225201218
536083BV00015B/764/P

9 781481 866613